We Came Here to Play

DAWN GRIFFIN

BALBOA.
PRESS

A DIVISION OF HAY HOUSE

Balboa Press books may be ordered through booksellers or by contacting:

Balboa Press
A Division of Hay House
1663 Liberty Drive
Bloomington, IN 47403
www.balboapress.com
1 (877) 407-4847

Because of the dynamic nature of the Internet, any web addresses or links contained in this book may have changed since publication and may no longer be valid. The views expressed in this work are solely those of the author and do not necessarily reflect the views of the publisher, and the publisher hereby disclaims any responsibility for them.

The author of this book does not dispense medical advice or prescribe the use of any technique as a form of treatment for physical, emotional, or medical problems without the advice of a physician, either directly or indirectly. The intent of the author is only to offer information of a general nature to help you in your quest for emotional and spiritual well-being. In the event you use any of the information in this book for yourself, which is your constitutional right, the author and the publisher assume no responsibility for your actions.

Any people depicted in stock imagery provided by Thinkstock are models, and such images are being used for illustrative purposes only. Certain stock imagery © Thinkstock.

Printed in the United States of America.

ISBN: 978-1-4525-1801-5 (sc)
ISBN: 978-1-4525-1803-9 (hc)
ISBN: 978-1-4525-1802-2 (e)

Library of Congress Control Number: 2014912099

Balboa Press rev. date: 07/09/2014

To the young ones who have chosen to come with their gifts at a time when both the challenges and the opportunities far outweigh what prior generations have had to deal with simultaneously.

As Buckminster Fuller said, "Our children and our grandchildren are our elders in universe time. They are born into a more complex, more evolved universe than we can experience or than we can know. It is our privilege to see that new world through their eyes."

Acknowledgements

It's ironic that this book was written on Ridgewood Ranch, the home of the famous racehorse, Seabiscuit, because this is also a story of hope in troubled times. There is love connected to the ranch that seems to call forth previously unnoticed gifts that were waiting to shine. It is with deepest gratitude that I thank the members of Christ Church of the Golden Rule for so generously supporting this offering of love, which is given on behalf of the Christ Consciousness in all of us.

With deepest appreciation also for my beloved mother, Pauline Griffin, whose faith in me helped this book to happen sooner than later. I also want to acknowledge the preliminary readers who gave me such supportive feedback, particularly Sandy Wold, Valerie Solheim, Kumu Keala Ching, Dave Wann, Sara Campbell and Rick Struble. Much love and appreciation to all! And, I can't conclude this without the affirmation of two unnamed angels who combed through the text to edit it to perfection.

Contents

Chapter 1

Acceleration

The time on Earth was intense. For those still fully in the dream, it was about struggle with a range of external conflicts. For those more ready to shift into a new story, the stumbling block was internal and stemmed from patterned conditioning and loyalty to mind as the only way to make sense of what was changing.

I came into this world to be Chris Carver, but that was only a half-truth and half-truths create confusion and an endless looping back of energy in an attempt to complete an interrupted circuit.

It's really all a game… and when you find the answer to your primary question you are ready to move on to the next level of play… Welcome to "the game."

The recounting of this story begins when I was a 16-year-old girl in foster care and I met a woman named Bree who saw through the protective facades I was hiding behind. One person who really sees you is all it takes to help you remember who you really are. Sometimes that one person just has to be yourself.

CHAPTER 2

Meeting Bree

A lot of what goes on with me is internal and it's hard for people to get me to talk about it. I'm perceived as a loner, but being seen is a funny thing. I believe we all want it, and I also choose who I'm willing to be visible with, because not everyone is ready to hold my offerings as sacred. Where I tell my story is in the sanctuary of the spoken word, with brothers and sisters, related by the blood of a larger truth. We are kindred spirits with many combinations of DNA, listening to each other for the deeper meaning, which was previously glossed over for convenience. We are reclaiming the art of elocution to turn sound bites into full meals that truly nourish.

Words hacked to pieces in text-speak are like junk food that doesn't satisfy any real need, and so we keep our fingers compulsively grabbing for more in hope of connection. As a society we are dealing with the consequences of not having time for more.

Bree is one of the only adults to have really *seen* me since the separation from my birth family. We met because we both have a passion for "spoken word," and we hang at an old beat-poetry coffee shop in Berkeley called The Beat Goes On, affectionately referred to as "The Beat," which has a weekly poetry slam. The walls are lined with old paper placemats scribbled with the musings of well-known beat poets from "back in the day" when protest and percussion merged to form a new genre of social commentary.

While most of the people who sign up to present in a "slam" are in their late teens to early twenties, there are a few people who are brave enough to make their offerings alongside the rawly honest, perceptive brilliance of the seasoned "slammers" who can unapologetically lay down the "word" and twirl their tongues back into their holsters still smokin. I was a novice word-slinger at fifteen when Bree first came in.

She knew that she was out of her league, as a middle-aged white woman who probably grew up with a Hallmark version of poetry, and a picture of the world that matched it. We all appreciated the way she would push her own limits without worrying about whether or not she fit in. No one cut her any slack either in the judging round, but that didn't matter because there was a sense that none of it was personal. It was just about being real... sharing truth without baggage... and the overall vibe of a slam is respect, empowerment and fun.

In that environment we are all pretty transparent with each other. Bree's focused attention on what we all had to share made me feel more open to getting to know her more. We have since developed a close relationship because she has a quiet, affirming presence that I haven't experienced since my mom died. She also doesn't seem to have any agenda with me, even though she is now my acting foster parent, after six months of jumping through hoops to get me from the family I had been with for two years. It's not common for Social Services to allow someone to take a kid from an established situation without evidence of abuse; and being restricted to the basement and not allowed to eat in the areas the rest of the family did, because I might mess things up, wasn't considered abuse. Do you know what it feels like when someone is always collecting evidence of every little thing you do wrong in order to build a case against you? Do you know what it's like to never be seen for the things you do that are efforts to follow "the rules"? Do you get why we stop trying?

A family can say they don't want you anymore, but choice is never an option on the side of the kid in question. My last family was worried about some of the words I used not being "family friendly." What does that mean anyway? "Darn it" just doesn't adequately express the emotion that comes up when it's being pointed out **again** that you've screwed up somehow. In my experience, "family friendly" is an oxymoron and it makes my stomach turn every time I hear it.

Many families who have foster kids do it for economic reasons and so petitioning to get me was like taking someone else's income source. They make an exception if you want to adopt a kid, which Bree was willing to do for me, but she didn't qualify because she was single, had insufficient income and was too old, even though she is one of those people who are so vital that age never seems to come into question. I don't know how she managed to pull off getting custody of me, but I'm glad she did, because with her I know it isn't about the money. I can tell that she really wants to be with me and that's a first since being in foster homes. Kind of crazy, if you ask me, that the people who really love and want you have to pay to get custody and the ones with no real interest in you are paid to take you.

I remember my first exchange with Bree. She came over to me at the end of one of the slams and she looked at me with those blue eyes and her black hair streaked with silver, pulled back off her face in a ponytail. The giant oval abalone earrings she was wearing had the most beautiful iridescent pattern of blues and turquoise, which brought out her eyes. There was something about her that just penetrated right into me.

"The piece you did really moved me," she said.

One of the things I liked about her initially was that she wasn't trying to be hip by dressing or talking like one of us. She was just being who she was and the way she spoke was natural to her.

"Can I sit down with you for a minute?" she asked.

"Ya, sure," I said matter-of-factly.

Then, seemingly out of the blue she said to me, "Sometimes things just seem to grab my attention as being important to share and I've learned to trust it. This might seem like an odd question, but do you know who Helen Keller was?"

"Ya, I've heard of her."

She continued, "But you may not know about the background of Annie Sullivan, the woman who came to be known as 'the miracle worker' for how she worked with Helen to free her from her dark, silent world."

"No, not really," I admitted, and only conveying minimal interest.

"You have a minute to hear it?" she asked.

"Ya, okay," I said.

Bree pulled back the empty, bentwood cane chair from the dimly-lit-corner table I was occupying and sat down, as the chair groaned a bit, revealing its age when she settled in. Her mug of chai was still steaming and she set it aside, as if she anticipated that it would be just right when she finished what she had to share.

She began, "Annie Sullivan's parents immigrated to the United States from Ireland during the Great Famine of the 1840s. The couple had five children, but two died in infancy.

Annie and her two surviving siblings grew up in impoverished conditions, and struggled with health problems. At the age of five, Annie contracted an eye disease called trachoma, which severely damaged her sight. Her mother, Alice, suffered from tuberculosis and had difficulty getting around after a serious fall. She died when Annie was eight years old.

Even at an early age, Annie had a strong-willed personality. She sometimes clashed with her father, Thomas, who was left to raise her and her siblings after their mother's death. Thomas—who was often abusive—eventually abandoned the family. Annie and her sick younger brother, Jimmie, were sent to live at the Tewksbury Almshouse, a home for the poor.

Tewksbury Almshouse was dirty, rundown, and overcrowded. It was known for its cruelty to inmates, because that's how they were treated, with poor European immigrants being the largest population of residents. Annie's brother Jimmie died just months after they arrived there, leaving her alone. She was known for her defiance, and as a result was caged in a dungeon for those labeled pauper insane and was treated like an animal because she would sometimes attack those who came near. Other times she would just sit in a daze.

There was, however, one older nurse who held out hope for all of God's children who would go down to the dungeon on her lunch break and sit quietly in the vicinity of Annie's enclosure, hoping to convey love to her. One day she left a brownie from her lunch next to Annie's cage, where she could reach it, and walked away. Annie acted as if she didn't notice, but the next time the nurse came down the brownie was gone, so she made it a practice to come down every Thursday with another offering.

As the weeks passed people began to notice a difference in Annie's behavior because one person had shown her kindness and eventually she was moved back upstairs. It was a total of four difficult years that Annie was at Tewksbury.

In an essay later published of her thoughts entitled, *Foolish Remarks of a Foolish Woman*, Annie stated: "I have endured much physical pain, and I can feel real pity for anyone who suffers. The misfortunes of the disinherited of the world rouse in me not only compassion but a fierce indignation."

The parallels in the story and my own life were eerie. I wondered what Bree knew about me and why she had chosen to tell me that story.

Bree went on, "The thing that breaks my heart the most is wasted potential and I see it all the time, including in myself. I wonder what it would be like on this planet if we got past our fear and claimed who we really are? "

Bree shifted gears slightly and asked me, "Do you know what you are here for?"

The question didn't come across as invasive, but it was unnervingly intriguing. No one ever asked questions like that in general conversation, especially in a first meeting. It certainly wasn't the kind of question I would ever find on a standardized test, where there was only one right answer.

I remember being a little wary and asking her, "Why are you so interested in me?"

"There's something familiar about you… a connection I can't walk away from, if I am paying attention. Sometimes you just know when someone else is linked to your purpose," Bree said in her unique way of meeting another person as an equal, regardless of age. She never talked to anyone younger like the adult with more experience and wisdom. She just looked at me in a disarming way like, I see who you are.

"I'd like to get to know you more. Maybe we could grab something to eat after one of the slams... on me," she added.

"Sure," I said, not knowing what to make of it all, but intrigued by whatever it was she perceived.

I also remember thinking that she would have liked my parents, and her heart would have ached over the potential that was lost there. Both my father and his brother had joined the Army back in 1996 and were shipped off to different conflicts in the Middle East. As African-American men they had hoped to find their way out of the poverty they had grown up in and to increase their chances of getting some trade skills and more than a high school education. My mother was a native Kurd that dad met when he was stationed in Kuwait. They had fallen in love pretty quickly, which I consider a sign of admirable character in the midst of so much fear, hatred and cultural difference.

I was born on December 12, 1999, toward the end of my dad's tour of duty, which was supposed to end in June 2000. He was discharged a few months early with non-fatal injuries that would plague him with both physical and emotional pain after he returned stateside with me and my mother, Delal, which meant beautiful, and she was. I still carry a picture of them, and as I get older I see myself more and more in the warmth of her hauntingly beautiful, brown eyes and chiseled cheekbones with olive skin.

They had planned to establish themselves in the East Bay area of California where my dad, Christopher, who I'm named after, grew up. His mother was alone and crippled from rheumatoid arthritis and was receiving assistance and living in bare-bones public housing. Uncle Frank wasn't lucky enough to make it home from Iraq, and dad felt it was important to keep what family there was together.

The return to the States felt like a fresh start away from a conflict zone, although as a black man the glasses he was looking through weren't quite as rosy as your average Joe. The 9/11 attack on the Twin Towers, which happened shortly after we were back in the country, didn't help matters any and, with my mom being Middle Eastern, we weren't warmly received by those wanting to be considered patriotic.

It seemed like things just went from bad to worse with dad having trouble getting and keeping jobs. The GI benefits weren't enough to support a family and help him get any additional schooling. He was also in a lot of physical discomfort and had turned to heroin when the prescription pain medication was cut off. In 2004, mom was diagnosed with ovarian cancer and, given the stress they were under and the marginal health care they had access to for her, she was gone by June of 2005. Dad and I ended up on the streets shortly after, but he was determined to keep me with him as motivation for turning his life around. Even though we moved from homeless shelter to homeless shelter, at least I knew I was still loved. I think wanting my dad to be okay was one of the reasons I grew up so fast. It wasn't more than six months of us being on the street when Social Services identified me for foster care. I was eight years old the last time I saw my father.

CHAPTER 3

Rebel without a Cause

My Pepe le Pew notification went off announcing I had a text by telling me that it was love at first sight. I figured the message was going to be from Bree, because by now the school would have contacted her to say I hadn't shown up for class.

"C, Wyd? School said u didn't show. Let me know ur ok. TTYL. ILY," the text message read.

"Was that Bree?" Brandon asked as we continued walking through the grove of oak trees now in full fall color, with a bit of fog still lingering as the warming rays of sun streamed gently through to disperse it.

"Ya," I said flatly.

"You gonna text her back?"

"Ya, in a minute," I said, as I paused, mesmerized by the glassy stillness of the lake reflecting a scene Monet must have borrowed.

The delay tactic was sort of a knee-jerk response to being kept on a short leash, although Bree never made me feel that way. Old habits die hard sometimes.

"I'm good. @ Tilden w B. TTYL. ILY2," I shot off in a reply.

Bree knows that Brandon Ino is my best friend and really nothing more. She also knows that we prefer the stimulating exchange of ideas in the open classroom at Tilden Park over the stagnant air in a formal classroom, which hadn't taken in any fresh energy in a long time. Bree shared the preference, and having access to this type of expansive nature is what made the modest, little two-bedroom apartment we shared workable.

Brandon is another slammer. A tall, lanky, Chinese American… brilliant and bored out of his mind in public school. I wish I had met him earlier because he is a senior now and finishing the credits he needs to graduate early, so he will be out of here by December. He doesn't cut class as often as I do, because he doesn't want the school to have any grounds for keeping him longer. He has plans to travel the world for a while after graduating to gather more experiences to inspire his poetry. On a day as glorious as today, though, he lets his arm be twisted.

Pepe le Pew's sweet voice summoned me again with another text… "no worries. Ur schl counslr wants to meet w both of us. I set it for Fri 9am. Work for u?"

"Ya," was all I replied, knowing I didn't have much choice.

"Is Bree out on a gig today?" Brandon asked.

"Ya, she's at a fundraiser for the Waldorf School in El Sobrante," I replied.

"You know there aren't too many people who can honestly say they live with a real clown," he chuckled.

"Well, not today. Today she's a fairy."

"Who would have ever dreamed you could make a living dressing up and playing with kids?" Brandon said somewhat amazed.

"Well, she doesn't totally make a living from it. She just says it gives her an excuse to be goofy and playful. She has a bag of tricks she pulls from for income including doing massage, cutting hair, quantum biofeedback and teaching English as a Second Language. All things that allow her to be somewhat mobile, at least until I came into the picture," I reflected, wondering if I was cramping her style.

"What's up with the school?" Brandon continued.

"I don't know. Last time we had a meeting it was because they were concerned that I was overly withdrawn and cutting too many classes."

"Just because you don't want to be assimilated?" Brandon laughed.

I joined him in making light of the whole bizarre scenario, but was also a little concerned about what they might recommend. Up to this point they hadn't been able to pinpoint a reason for medicating me. I wasn't ADHD or hyperactive, but they may try to play the antidepressant card. There had, after all, been an increase in the suicide rate at the school, particularly among girls.

Brandon was awesome with impromptu commentary on most any subject and he launched in with his portrayal of a teacher giving a lecture on "clonization." He motioned to the flock of ducks quietly gliding across the water in our direction, who were most likely coming to see if we had brought bread crumbs or other offerings.

"Now pay attention students. Today's lecture is on Clonization. Please do not take notes because this will not be on the final exam. It is actually just a test to see if you still have any independent reasoning skills intact.

If you do, we will identify them and design a curriculum to systematically dismantle them.

Curiosity will get you nothing but trouble and creativity is really overrated.

The systems you need to be safe have all been put in place for you.

Unless of course, one of you snaps, and it that case it's wise to be armed.

We will be adding responsible firearm use to next year's course offerings.

Please put your cell phones away. I do know that you are texting because my lecture isn't entertaining enough to warrant the grins on your faces and neither are your crotches."

As Brandon concluded his entertaining jag we both fell into hysterics. That's why I love him... he is a great antidote to life and I hated the thought of him going away so soon after we met.

"Hey," Brandon said, "Have you seen the movie, *Brave?*"

"No"

"Wanna watch it before Bree gets home today? I have a copy of it. It's one of my favorite movies," he said with that familiar twinkle in his eye.

Even though I hadn't seen the film, I knew it wasn't a typical "guy" film. It was one of the things that made him so cool to me. He was just cut from a different cloth, as my dad used to say about me.

"Sounds great. Is it at your house?" I asked.

"Ya, we can swing by there and grab it and also snag some falafels at the Pita Pit on the way back to your place. Does that work for you?" Brandon queried.

"Sounds like a plan!"

Brandon had the car and we had the "smart" HDTV, which Bree had given in to buying last year when she realized it would be a useful tool for augmenting my education. I spent a fair amount of time watching PBS programming as a part of my agreement with Bree. I also surfed youtube for spoken word and music videos, and when Brandon was over he would rope me into a game of *Minecraft*.

Brandon took off to go home just before Bree arrived back at the apartment at four thirty. I could tell she was tired after a day of being chased through a magical garden by a mob of energetic kids, more than she was upset with me. I was feeling fantastic after a wonderfully stimulating day and would have been unapologetic about having missed a day of school, if Bree had tried to go there with me.

"Hey, Chris…" was all Bree could summons as she plopped herself into the overstuffed leopard print velour chair in the living room. "I just need about an hour to decompress, have a cup of tea and get out of this fairy outfit and then I think it would be good to talk. Does that work for you?"

"Yaaaa, whatever," I said in a drawn out way to indicate it wasn't me who wanted to have the conversation.

"And, if you're gonna get serious with me I think it makes sense that you not be wearing the fairy outfit," I added with a well-intended sarcasm.

Bree managed to muster a grin in appreciation, her eyes still closed and her legs splayed over the matching leopard print ottoman.

I went out onto the deck of our second-floor apartment to absorb the warmth of the late afternoon sun. Bree had managed to cram as many plants as possible around the periphery of the modest deck to create a continuum between the Earth-tone stucco walls of our complex and the surrounding wooded hills. She had a way of creating flow and had dabbled in Feng Shui, which I had come to appreciate. There was a sense of overall ease in the apartment that Brandon and others who visited also commented on.

The hour had been absorbed by the day, just as the warm sun had been taken into my bones. Bree slid the glass door open and poked her head out looking renewed.

"Wanna talk out here?" she asked softly, not sure if she should disturb my peace.

"Sure," I said.

She walked out and pulled one of the patio chairs over and sat down next to me. I had closed my eyes again to continue basking, but she knew I was listening.

"Chris, I get why you don't want to be in class at your school. I also know that as a foster parent I can't get too outside of the box with what I let you do, or Social Services could determine I'm not an appropriate care provider," Bree began. "So, we need to come up with a plan that is going to help you get through these last couple of years as easily as possible."

She continued, "I know you know what you don't want, but what's more important in changing the situation is focusing on what you do want, so let's talk about that."

"I don't really know what other options I have," I said, having been over this question in my own mind a thousand times.

"Well, let's say that your school situation remains as it is, but you have a goal outside of that, which inspires you," Bree suggested.

"Like what?" I said with a tone of exasperation.

"Like joining Brandon on an international adventure after you graduate," Bree threw out as a possibility.

"Ya, right, like how am I going to do that?" I shot back, a little frustrated. I want a **real** solution **now**, I thought to myself.

"Okay, so you know that I was married in my early twenties," Bree said, as I could see her building her case. "Well, Mark and I were both working at sort of boring jobs, but we were accepting it as just part of life. Then we went to see a travel show on Europe put on by Kodak Cameras. I was particularly moved by it and really wanted to go. Mark loved the show too, but had never considered it a possibility because we were young and just getting started and didn't have the money to do it.

I said to Mark, what if we just say we are going and start checking into everything that needs to happen to get us there. He started warming up to the idea, so we committed in our minds to make the journey the following spring. We got our passports. We bought backpacks and would put stuff in them and walked around the little neighborhood park every night after dinner to get used to carrying them, and while we did that we imagined and talked about all of the places we would go. We also picked up extra jobs in the evenings and weekends selling tickets at sporting events and saved everything we made from that. As the reality of leaving approached we decided we would both give notice on our jobs and find new ones when we came back, because we wanted to travel for nine weeks and we thought it was unlikely we could get a leave of absence for that amount of time. To our surprise both of our employers gave us leaves of absence when we told them why we were quitting."

By the time Bree concluded, I was starting to feel the excitement of what it would be like to be on a big adventure with Brandon, but what if he didn't think that was such a great idea? Before I could even get this picture blown up in my mind I started deflating my own balloon.

"Brandon will have already been traveling for a year and a half by time I'm out of school. It's not like I'm his girlfriend either and he may have hooked up with someone he really likes," I started rationalizing. "Not to mention how I would ever come up with the money to do that."

"Okay, okay," Bree said, "so maybe it's not Brandon, or maybe it's not traveling around the world, but find something that really makes you happy when you think about it. I'm not talking about what you want to do for the rest of your life, just something that gets you excited when you think about doing it. Then figure out what you need to do to make it happen, as if it's possible. Got it?... which means stop looking for all the reasons it probably wouldn't work."

"In the meantime, we need to come up with a plan for the meeting tomorrow morning with Mr. Sarcucci, who I'm sure is going to want to address the number of times you've cut class. Even though your grades are still decent, they can use that as reason to hold you back, and the last thing you want to do to yourself is to extend your stay in high school, right? So work with me on this," Bree implored.

Damn, she is always so reasonable, I thought to myself when all I really wanted to do was just rebel against the whole crazy system. I took a deep sigh and surrendered, "Okay, whaddya got?"

"So, you know the anonymous love letters I started writing after seeing the TED talk by that young woman who was looking for an antidote to her depression by writing love letters to strangers?" Bree reminded me.

"Ya," I said, curious about where she was going with this.

"Well, you can get extra credit for civic projects, right?" she continued.

"Ya."

"Okay, so what if you propose starting a project in your school to get students to write anonymous love letters that could be collected and given to the local Meals On Wheels office to have randomly delivered by their drivers to the people who are shut-in? Who knows maybe it would inspire people who have received the letters to write letters of their own to make someone else's day better and it could start generating a supply of letters from within the Meals On Wheels community. Maybe it is also an antidote to depression for the students who write the letters, just as it was for the young woman who started the project."

Bree was letting it all land and then concluded, "You're a communicator, Chris, and I know you're good at writing."

"Ya, but I don't know what I would say to a stranger to make their day," I said, feeling the resistance rise in me.

"Do you know who you are speaking to when you write your poetry?... No, you just say what's real for you in a way that gets people to pay attention and think differently. It's not about syrupy-sweet greetings. It's about being kind and remembering to see people who've gone off our radar. Think about things people have said or done for you at times when you were in a tough space, or that you wish someone had done, and be the one to offer it." Bree had made her case and now it was up to the jury of one... me.

"Why don't you sit with it overnight and, if you come up with another idea that feels more right for you, then by all means present that tomorrow. I'm just trying to be proactive, so we aren't in a position of having to accept Mr. Sarcucci's recommendations."

"I know, Bree, and I appreciate it. So, what do I say if he asks me what the inspiration was for the project?... a fairy?"

We both ripped a snorting laugh as we agreed that might not be the best idea, if we hoped to avoid being pressured on the medication issue.

The next morning we didn't have any discussion before heading over to Mr. Sarcucci's office for the scheduled meeting. When we arrived, we each took a seat in one of the cold, vinyl chairs outside his office and the nervous tension was the same as anticipating any other kind of examination.

Mr. Sarcucci was actually a man with a gentle disposition, although he had to also convey authority. His stature wouldn't do that because he was a smaller built man with a thin frame. His graying hair was either premature, or he was just a man whose years weren't reflected in his vibrant skin tone.

"Good morning, Chris. Good morning, Ms. Blakely," he said as he came out of his office. He was obviously hoping to set an upbeat tone for what could be an uncomfortable discussion. He gestured toward his office, allowing us to go first.

"So, I know your probably aware of what this meeting is for, since this isn't the first time we've addressed the issue of cutting class and being socially withdrawn," Mr. Sarcucci began, obviously wanting to cut to the chase and come up with a solution.

"Chris, I want you to know that your well-being and success at this institution is our priority."

As I looked at him, all I could see where the words "blah, blah, blah" in a cartoon bubble coming off his head and I tried to tune back in so he couldn't use this as further evidence of my being withdrawn.

"While your grades aren't really an issue, you are in violation of the number of unexcused absences allowed for passing you through to eleventh grade, and we aren't even half way through the year. Also, your lack of participation in class when you are here makes me a little concerned that depression may be an issue. As you know, teenage suicide, particularly among girls, is on the rise and we would like to see you get the help you need. I am going to recommend that you see a psychiatrist of your own choosing, or one that we can refer, to get an assessment," he concluded, in an open and shut manner.

I noticed Bree having trouble biting her tongue as Mr. Sarcucci read from his notes without even looking up.

"With all due respect, Mr. Sarcucci, Chris, and I'm sure most of the other "at-risk kids" whose well-being you have in mind, have a lot to be depressed about in the world right now and I don't believe the antidote is to medicate them so they become normalized to the insanity. I think you would be better served to give them a voice and the tools they need to create *real* solutions for their future," Bree said with a fierce clarity that left Mr. Sarcucci speechless.

Smoke was still venting from Bree's ears, when I stood up and placed a piece of paper on Mr. Sarcucci's desk. Bree looked at me quizzically, wondering what I was up to.

"Mr. Sarcucci, this is a proposal for a civic project, which I believe will offset the days missed from class this year. I've written up the details of it to give you time to digest the overall benefit for myself and other students at the school, as well as the larger community. Shall we set another meeting to discuss the details of it, if it meets with your approval?" I said, feeling the joy of using my gift for spoken word in a new venue, backed by Bree's unwavering belief in me.

Mr. Sarcucci was still trying to collect himself after he had been blown out by both Bree and me. "Uh, sure," he stammered. "Let me take a look at this and my calendar and get back to you."

"That sounds good," Bree said. "We'll show ourselves out."

As we left the room, it must have felt like the sucking out of all the air after a tornado has passed through. When we got outside into the parking lot we turned to each other and simultaneously high-fived, "You Rock!"

CHAPTER 4

Know What You Want

Two weeks after our meeting with Mr. Sarcucci to address the threat of my being held back a year, and rerouting a train headed toward *Paxil*, Bree and I found ourselves back in his office, anticipating a favorable outcome. This time he received us more like a businessman ready to negotiate a deal than a politician shaking hands and kissing babies as a way to win our compliance.

"Good to see you both again," he said, with a serious tone that said, I'm ready for you this time.

He held the door to his office open and motioned for us to have a seat. He pulled himself to the oak desk that looked like it had been there since the founding of the school in 1950, then he cleared his throat, beginning, "Chris, I'm impressed with the proposal you presented and I am prepared to accept it, if you agree to the following terms."

He pulled a paper from the file folder and started down the list. "I propose we make this a two-month project, which will take us to the end of this year. Assuming you have not cut more classes, that will be sufficient to put you back in good standing for successfully completing your sophomore year.

You will need to provide me with documentation for the file by having someone at Meals On Wheels sign off that they have received the letters each week and how many. I would suggest that it not be fewer than five letters a week. To be honest, I think it would be wonderful if you can inspire others to join you, because I do see the benefit of this project both for the students that participate and the larger community, if it takes off. Are those terms you can agree to?"

Bree looked over at me as if to say, the ball is in your court. I knew that it was that or back to square one with how to avoid being held back a year. I had gotten her point the other night about finding the best way through these remaining years, rather than digging a hole for myself I would later regret.

"Ya, that's good," I said feeling relieved, but not yet as excited as Bree was about the project.

The rest of the meeting seemed like a blur, as I found myself thinking about how I was just drifting through life, letting my future be determined by what someone else handed me to deal with, and not expecting much in terms of real satisfaction.

Bree squeezed me on the shoulder as she stood up and made an extended reach over Mr. Sarcucci's desk to shake his hand. I tuned back in and grabbed the backpack and hoodie I had set on the floor next to my chair and sort of nodded and mumbled, "thanks," as I stood and turned toward the door with Bree right behind me.

When we got into the hallway outside the counseling office, the school day was in full swing with students shuffling through lockers, milling around the vending machines and texting each other as they navigated to class seemingly oblivious of what was going on around them, but managing to avoid collisions, nonetheless.

Bree and I split off in different directions… she headed toward the parking lot and I went on to history class. Before she got too far away, though, she turned in my direction and yelled over to me, "Hey Chris, let's celebrate tonight."

Not turning back around, I raised my fist in a "power to the people" sort of gesture that let Bree know I was down with that. I didn't really have a lot of friends in the school and I always acted like I didn't care what any of them thought anyway, so why the cool façade? I guess some things are just a mystery. Partly, my mind was spinning on the point Bree had made the other night about identifying something that would make me happy and focusing on that instead of what I don't want.

Bree always encourages me to be the cause of my life rather than at the effect of it, and hearing the stories she shares about her numerous adventures is chipping away at the resignation I have that life is just hard and that I have no real power to change it.

I arrived at my history class and slid into a chair at the back of the room, hoping not to be called on. They could require my body to be present, but it was really hard to stay focused on the one-sided, white-male version of battles and exploitations, or as the teacher put it, explorations. The one benefit of the class was that it did provide some good content for social commentary poetry.

It was getting close to the end of the school day when my phone vibrated to let me know a text had come in. I figured it was Bree checking in about tonight and it was.

"C, am @ an estate sale near school this aft. Can pick U up 4 early dinner @ Riyadh's. How bout the usual spot?"

Getting picked up was more of a rarity. Usually I'd catch a bus or sometimes grab a ride with Brandon. When I did get picked up, the usual spot was on the side of the school, which was an easier in and out with the mass exodus of cars from the main parking lot at the end of the day. Any of the routes would be congested, but that one tended to be the best.

I sent a quick reply before dashing into my last class of the day, "Ya. See U L8r."

Riyadh's was one of our favorite Lebanese restaurants with really fresh traditional food and an oven on the back brick wall of the main dining area, where you could see the open flame through the glass window and watch the chefs attentively prepare their delicacies on the other side. Just the thought of the freshly baked breads made my mouth water. It also brought up memories of my mom making beautiful, simple food for us, even up until just before she died. It was something she loved doing and it was an important part of holding together a sense of family as things fell apart. Bree appreciated the importance of the practice for me and had always made a point to sit down to at least one meal together a day without the distractions of smart phones, notebooks or the TV.

The last hour of the school day flew by, despite the frustration of being in Mr. Green's geometry class and trying to follow what he was explaining with his stutter, which turned the isosceles triangle into an issss-sssoss-ceeleeesssse triii-annn-gle.

As the final bell rang, I gathered my things quickly and made my way out the door through a cheer squad gathering to practice their routines in the grassy area on the side of the building where Bree was meeting me.

I heard, "Toot-toot" and could see it was Tinkerbell, Bree's iridescent blue Ford Fiesta hybrid, the color of dragonfly wings. Bree always names everything because she says it is all energy and when you treat it with love and appreciation it works better.

I wasn't about to argue because her whacky ways just seemed to work somehow. In a crazy way, Bree was one of the most childlike people I had ever known. She just seemed to approach life with a sense of awe and appreciation, and delighted in finding ways to make a game of it all. She would say that, "Things are not always what they appear to be," and "I love being surprised by how it's all connected."

She seemed so naïve to me at times and I realized how fast I had grown up in response to tough circumstances. I couldn't justify making "a game" out of life, but then Bree would tell me about someone like the woman who was the oldest living Nazi concentration camp survivor at age 110, and how she was still beaming about the beauty of life and her appreciation for the music that had sustained her. I still wasn't willing to use the word "game" to describe life, but I could accept that our experiences have a lot to do with attitude and choice.

When I first came up against this aspect of Bree, I resented her privileged, white Pollyanna-isms, thinking that she had no idea what it was like to be a person of color in a world that marginalized, feared and tried to control anyone resembling a pigment of the Earth. She would always sense the friction as I pushed up against her, as the generic face of oppression; but, rather than let me give my power away as a victim, she would ask me how my circumstances had contributed to the exceptional person that I am. One time she had said, "I care about you too much to relate to you as not enough in some way. You can argue for your limitations, but I never will. Claim who you really are and speak truth to it."

I remember when Bree first asked me if I would like to come and live with her, and I said, "What makes you think that you can understand my reality, let alone change it?"

She responded, "I don't pretend to really understand your reality, because I'm not in your skin, nor is anyone else, even those who fall into a similar category of life experience. At the same time, you can't know what it is to be in my skin, so to think you understand what motivates me is also presumptive. I may be imperfectly compassionate, but at least it is my intention to grow in that capacity and, if I'm going to put this much effort into it, I'm going to choose someone who has the ability to match me in the endeavor...

...It isn't so much about changing your reality as much as it is about changing the collective reality, because all of our liberation is bound up together. Sometimes it's the ones with seemingly nothing left to lose who end up showing us what we are really made of."

When I reached the curb where Bree was parked, I pulled the back, passenger-side door of Tinkerbell open and threw my backpack in before getting in the front seat.

"Be careful of the armillary sphere," Bree said.

"The **what?**" I said, wondering what Bree was up to now.

"That thing," she said as she pointed to the brass, spherical framework of rings centered around an orb, which was sitting in the back seat. "Get in and I'll tell you about it."

"So what is that thing called and what is it for?" I asked again, as I settled in the car.

"It's a 16th century, French armillary sphere, also called a spherical astrolabe. It's a model of objects in the sky that represent lines of celestial longitude and latitude and other astronomically important features such as the ecliptic," Bree explained, as if she were an authority on the subject.

"What's an ecliptic?" I interrupted.

"I don't know yet," Bree confessed, "but it will make for a great science project. Maybe we can figure out how it works. If not, it will look great on the deck in the garden and will be a fantastic conversation piece," she mused. "Anyway, it was the prime instrument used by all astronomers in determining celestial position, prior to the advent of the European telescope in the 17th century."

"Is that what you went to the estate sale for?" I asked, thinking how much more interesting this was than the history and science classes I had earlier.

"I didn't know what I might discover when I went to the sale, but this was a real score. I'm thinking they must have sold it for a fraction of what it's worth. More cause to celebrate tonight," Bree said with delight.

"Hey, Bree, I know that redeeming myself with the school is reason to celebrate, and I do like your idea, but I'm just not as excited about it as you are," I confessed.

"I know," Bree said, "but it's only for two months and, because I love writing the anonymous love letters, I will contribute the ones I write to your cause. I also want to apologize for not giving you more time to come up with your own awesome solution before I scheduled that initial meeting."

She shifted gears a little and continued, "So, what is it that you **are** really excited about that we are celebrating tonight?"

"How do you know there is something I'm excited about?" I asked, curious about what Bree was tuning into.

"You usually have something cookin in your head when you are off in never-never land like you were this morning. Anyway, as Dr. Seuss's Lorax might say, *I am the Listener, I interpret the needs*," she laughed, appreciating her own word play. I have to hand it to Bree for being willing to delight in herself, whether anyone else did or not.

"Okay, well, did you see the posting at The Beat about the annual *Brave New Voices Festival* that's going to be held in Chicago in August?" I asked.

"Yes," Bree said.

"I want to get on a team and qualify to compete there."

"Awesome," Bree said, "and how appropriate that after dinner I am taking you to the Trans-Parent Poet in San Francisco, where that festival was launched. Since we are having dinner early, we will be able to make it for the slam tonight."

What could I say... I just pushed the car seat back as far as it would go, grinned and propped my loosely laced, purple high tops, complemented by a pair of rainbow stripped leggings against the dashboard.

Dinner at Riyadh's was like hanging out with family because we frequented the place so often. It was family owned and operated and the smells and the generous servings of warmth and hospitality alone were worth the visit. As we walked in the door we were greeted by Mahdi, the son, whose name means "guided to the right path." He had a natural way of putting people at ease and guiding them to the right table. He, of course, knew where our favorite spot was.

"Hey, you're here early today," he said, not even bothering to grab menus, because we pretty much had the offerings memorized.

"Ya, we are headed over to San Fran for a poetry slam tonight, so we can't hang here as long as we would like," I said, conveying both genuine warmth and an aloofness that would keep Bree from zeroing in on my broader interest in Mahdi.

Some of the days when I had skipped classes, I would come over here alone for lunch just so I could hang out around him. He never asked me why I wasn't in school. He was just cool, and I'm sure he picked up on my interest, but he always kept it light and respectful. Besides, he is probably at least twenty and he has a girlfriend that comes in to see him sometimes. He's just so much more together than most of the guys at school and his attractiveness to me is a combination of his warmth, self-assurance and easy manner with people, along with his toned body, olive skin and green eyes, like those of a tiger, and his thick-black-tousled hair. The combination of attributes conveyed self-respect more than ego.

"Cool," Mahdi said, with a tone of genuine interest. "I know you do spoken word too, Chris, and I'd love to bring my girlfriend, Sarah, over to The Beat sometime for one of the slams. Text me when you are signed up to perform and we'll try and catch it, if it's not a night I'm working." He scribble down his email address on a sheet of the order tablet and handed it to me.

"Awesome, I will," was all I said, trying not to let on to just how awesome that really was and also how it made me a little nervous to think about him being in the audience.

Because we were here ahead of the normal dinner rush, the restaurant was still pretty quiet, so Mahdi also took our orders. "Do you want to know what the specials are today?" he asked.

"I would," Bree said.

"Okay, well, the soup of the day is a lentil soup with spinach and lemon. As an entrée we are offering a baked red snapper with sumac and oregano spices, and we also have a Mankoushé with olive oil, fresh tomato, cucumber, goat chèvre, pine nuts and mint, which is a Lebanese pizza.

"The snapper sounds delicious," Bree said, "I'll have that."

"I want the pizza," I said, "and a mango lassi."

"What about for you to drink, Bree?"

"Pomegranate tea, thanks!"

Mahdi's parents Ihsan and Bashira, were busy in the kitchen with prep work when they saw through the glass window in the open-wall oven that we had come in. Whenever it wasn't too crazy busy they would come out personally with a little extra offering to keep us busy while the main dishes were being prepared. Tonight they came out with garlic naan just out of the oven and hummus.

"So how are two of our favorite people doing tonight?" Ihsan asked, as he laid a welcoming hand against my shoulder.

"Really good," I said, "We're on our way to an awesome slam."

Bashira, like a concerned mother said, "That's good, I hope."

Ihsan added, "It's hard for us to keep up with all the changes in the world. That's why we stick with food. People will always need to eat and it's a language that doesn't change that much."

We all laughed, and they went back to their respective tasks.

After eating our food, we didn't linger as long as we might have. You never know what you are going to run into with traffic in the Bay area and we didn't want to miss any of the slam. The traffic gods seemed to be with us, however, and we made it comfortably to the Trans-Parent Poet on time.

While I usually preferred a stealthy table in a dimly lit back corner, tonight I wanted to be front and center to study every nuance of the spoken word artists, who could leave an audience stunned and speechless. Bree and I found a table just back of where the stage spotlights made the audience visible. The Emcee for the event was poised and engaging, as if he was born for this. He couldn't have been more than 22 years old, yet the impromptu wit and appreciative rhetoric lavished on each contestant, turned this otherwise geek-seeming-thick-black-framed-glasses-string bean into an oratory God.

The last slammer of the night particularly spoke to me. She was probably only a couple of years older than me, black as could be and beautiful beyond belief. Her cornrowed hair had strands of gold woven into it and it hung halfway down her back. She had a gold loop eyebrow piercing over her left eye and a diamond stud in her right nostril. Her soulful brown eyes caught the glint of the spotlight when she would move her head just right, and sparks seemed to fly from them to accentuate the precisely placed words. Her clothes were edgy and arty, and adorned her beautifully rounded body as a temple rather than putting it on display as cheap wares for sale.

I was spellbound as she began,

> Who am I to feel that I should be free to create
> to laugh,
> to live,
> to love,
> unrestrained by rules that someone else thought up
> to give meaning to lives grown stagnant,
> and to make certain that which cannot be known.
>
> I am but one beat in the heart of life,
> one sweet breath of the Earth taken in
> that I may serve to sustain her.
> Let this be my awareness,
> lest I forget to use this moment well.

As such, I have no need for a system in which
the consumer becomes the consumed.
Insidious messages delivered by a handmaiden of fear
beckoning all down a path of unfulfilled desires.

Will there ever be enough?
Enough time,
youth slipping away.
Enough money,
to keep up with it all.
Enough love,
partners and offspring,
assets held in reserve
accumulating no interest.

After the final judging round, Bree and I peeled ourselves off the chairs we had been glued to all night and floated out of the coffee shop, moved and mesmerized. We walked silently back to the car, obviously more than satisfied with the summation of the celebration the universe had delivered.

We were probably no more than fifteen minutes from home when we passed through a green light, only to have Tinkerbell swatted around by a texting driver who was more interested in the Instagram photo of his drunken friends at the party he had just left, than the red light in front of him. The smack to the backside of the car spun us around and up over the curb, which was fortunately unoccupied at that moment. The airbags had inflated to keep us both from being projected through the windshield, but the armillary sphere went airborne and nailed me in the left side of the head because I still had the seat pushed all the way back.

I heard Bree's voice, as if through a distant tunnel, scream, "Chris…" and then I was hovering in between two very different realities.

CHAPTER 5

Dimensional Shift

Emergency vehicle lights were flashing everywhere and I was aware of every aspect of the chaos on the scene. Bree was next to me holding my hand as they loaded me into the ambulance. I was trying to talk to Bree to tell her everything was fine, but no words were coming out of my mouth and everyone was talking about me as if I wasn't there.

"We still have vitals, but they are low. She has a TBI and is unconscious and we need to get her to the hospital right away to monitor her for brain swelling," the young, but very efficient and confident male paramedic explained to Bree, as the driver swung the back doors closed with everyone on board and sped off.

Bree mumbled quietly, not knowing that I could hear her, "This was supposed to be a celebration, Chris. Damn it. You have too much to offer to leave now. The world needs you, so get that brilliant, defiant ass of yours back here."

I was in some sort of "expanded" reality. I wasn't seeing the tunnel I had heard so many people talk about who had had near death experiences, but it was like I was seeing everything from every perspective, as if I was all of it, including animals and "inanimate objects." It was like being one continuous stream of thought changing forms to comply to **its** wishes, whatever **it** was. I also felt the most incredible peace I could ever imagine and there was no judgment about any of what was happening in the space. There also wasn't any hook to pull me to identify with those who were struggling or suffering, nor an attachment to move in the direction of those in ecstatic states elsewhere. It all just **was**... equally... and there was a profound, euphoric sense of wellbeing that felt nothing like what I had identified as love. That is, in terms of a feeling I associated with people who made me feel good about myself or about life. It was love as prime cause of the universe. In this moment, I knew awareness only and "myself" had no meaning.

Then the thought came, **you have to make a choice**, and I remembered the question Bree asked me when we first met, "Do you know why you are here?"

I felt my identification as the body lying in that hospital bed, hooked up to monitors, let go and a surge of energy passed through the unresponsive hand Bree was still clinging to and went into her body like a reset button removing fear and any sense of potential loss. She lingered in that blissful state, appreciative of what she could only call grace, and then leaned over, kissed me on the forehead and softly said, "Travel well, dear one. I am always with you."

Bree walked out of the ICU room and said to the nurse who was seated at the desk and monitoring all of the critical patients, "I'm going home to rest. There's not much else I can do here now and it could be quite a while before she comes out of the coma."

The nurse knew that Bree had also been in the accident. It was midnight now and she was concerned that Bree might not be up to getting herself home.

"If you want to sleep here tonight, I can set a cot up in the room with her," the nurse said.

Bree thought about how her neck was throbbing from the whiplash, and that it would mean getting a cab, since she didn't even know where her car might have been taken or whether it was even drivable. She still opted for the inconvenience of coordinating a way home at a late hour, over an uncomfortable cot with cold, fluorescent lights on all night. She also had some alternative healing devices at home that she knew would help more than anything else.

"I'll be okay, but thanks for the kindness," Bree said, and she pulled her cell phone out of her purse to call a cab. She had always had an aversion to hospitals with their stringent sterility and absence of anything that energetically felt like life, but as she walked toward the front of the hospital to catch the cab, there was a pervasive sense of peace.

* * *

I was in some sort of large green opalescent plasma tube, which I experienced as a heightened sensory awareness. It was like being in the center of a hologram—seeing everything around me, but not with my physical eyes. It felt alive with an energy I can only describe as unconditional love and being swaddled in total comfort and safety. There were scenes from various time periods playing out simultaneously, and I had the sense that I was a character in all of them. Some of the scenes were gruesome, some were glorious and none of them seemed to really matter, other than being momentarily entertained in a movie I had purchased a ticket for.

Then everything seemed to slow and I felt a warm liquid around my body. My head was back and I was floating. As I opened my eyes, I saw water flowing down a stepped-rock formation of various red and yellow hues. There was a canyon mouth up behind the pour over, which gaped wide, revealing the inner mysteries of Earth that had given way to the sculpting aspects of moving water.

I was in some kind of thermal pool on the canyon floor below. It was the deepest sense of being cleansed, as if I had just emerged into the world from this great mother, innocent and uncluttered. The landscape was unfamiliar on one level, and at the same time I dropped into it like resting in the arms of a cradling elder.

I realized my body was naked in the pool, which felt natural and sacred, as if I had just been baptized. I had no sense of where I was, nor did I feel any urgency to figure it out. There was total silence, in human terms, although the water burbled down the rock face above and I felt like I could hear the steam rising from the pool I was in. I swear I could also hear the gnawing of leaves by ants busily working in the area. Great black birds' wings whooshed as they climbed to catch and ride the thermals above, occasionally cawing to announce their presence. It was an incredible symphony to my ears. It seemed I had gotten an upgrade to my hearing and other senses as well. I let the warmth of the late afternoon sun and the mineral water pool speak to my cells of all that really matters.

There was a towel, a glass of water, and a piece of clothing on the ground next to the pool, which seemed to be left for me, as if I were a patron at a spa. When I felt inclined to move from this initiating womb, I reached over and drank the glass of cool, refreshing water. Then I easily climbed from the warmth of the shallow spring and dried myself off. I slipped the simple, but elegant, ivory colored chemise of finely woven hemp and silk over my head and it draped and clung to my body like corn silk over a cob.

As I slowly did a three-sixty to take in the breathtakingly beautiful expanse, I noticed a man sitting near an unusual grouping of rock spires with flat rocks capping each one, giving the appearance of a gathering of ancient beings holding circle. He was about a football field's distance away and his gaze was fixed in the direction of the horizon the sun was moving toward. He was dressed in khaki pants and a basic, heather gray sleeveless t-shirt with a red, paisley bandana tied around his neck. His glossy, long black hair was pulled back off his face at the temples, with the lower portion hanging down between the blades of his broad shoulders.

He looked approachable and I had a million questions about where I am and how I had gotten here. I hadn't really thought about not having shoes on until I started walking in his direction. It wasn't discomfort that made me notice, which I would have expected, since I wasn't used to walking without shoes, but there was a heightened awareness of vibration coming up through the soles of my feet that seemed to translate into images of geometric patterns flashing across my mind. It was confusing and I didn't know what to make of it. As soon as I had the thought of it being too much information, it subsided and I could refocus on the man, who I was now about ten yards away from.

Feeling my approach, he turned to face me. His face was serene and welcoming, the smile more in his penetrating brown eyes, than on his full lips. His characteristics were a blend of something, maybe Native and African American, with high cheekbones, a prominent brow and a broad nose. I could also see that he had tattoos that ringed his biceps in a chain of symbols that felt like some sacred code. He felt energetically like one of the stone, Earth elders he was sitting in council with… deep, solid, and a silent observer.

"They are called hoodoos," he said.

"Who what?" I said, thrown off by the unusual introduction.

"You were thinking about these rock formations," he said gesturing toward the upward thrusting spires. "They are called, hoodoos, h-o-o-d-o-o-s," he said, spelling it out.

"How did you know that's what I was thinking?" I responded, one eyebrow raising to reflect the question.

"Ah, yes," the mystery man began, "basically, things are much more transparent here and much of our communication is telepathic. If you can hold **that** thought for a moment and the multitude of others following it, I will be happy to answer all of them in due time."

"So what's **that** thought you are suggesting I hold?" I curiously inquired.

"Where's **here** and who are you, meaning me?" he said, as he pointed to himself. "So, first things first, my name is Trevor, and you are in a national conservation area known as the Escalante."

Trevor continued, "Since you have so many questions and they are firing pretty much simultaneously, I will invite you to ask them in the order that makes the most sense to you. Otherwise, I have to spend a bit of time untangling them; and being conversational will feel more natural to you anyway."

"I'm not sure anything here feels exactly natural at the moment, but you're right that I have so many questions it's hard to know where to start," I said, taking a deep breath to get myself more present in my body and receptive to what Trevor had to say.

"I think the biggest question has to do with why I am **here**? I mean, it feels like I am still in my body and on the Earth somewhere, so I'm not getting that I died."

"You're right," Trevor began, "you didn't die in the way you think about death, meaning that you completely give up the physical form you occupy through a certain lifetime and it's over. Let's just say you switched channels temporarily."

"I'm not exactly following you yet," I said with a perplexed look on my face.

"Okay, let me ask you a question," he said, "What did you experience when you came through what I will call a time-space wormhole?"

"So, you know how I got here?"

"Yes."

"No surprise, I guess. That must be why the towel, the water and this piece of clothing were conveniently next to the hot spring pool," I said, as I looked down at what I was wearing.

"Yes, well I presumed you would prefer that to the hospital gown you were last seen in," he said, making light of the situation. "Anyway, back to my question. What do you remember coming through the tube?"

"It was like watching a movie screen with multiple scenes from very different stories playing out simultaneously, yet it felt like there was a common thread running through all of them," I replied.

"What did the common thread feel like?" Trevor said, as he continued his exploration with me.

"Like I was the actor in all of the scenes… like I was watching myself."

"Good," Trevor said, "that's a good place to start. Basically, you are in the same physical form, but you are in a higher frequency dimension… a parallel reality, temporarily. Your physical capacities are expanded and function on a more subtle level. Everything will feel lighter and you will know yourself more as pure energy than dense matter."

"Yes, I've noticed that already with my hearing and information coming through my feet. The energy here does feel different. It's more electric… sort of super charged and energizing, but at the same time deep and still."

I looked down at Trevor's feet and noticed he was not wearing shoes either. "So, no one wears shoes here?" I asked.

"Well, primarily it's the 'Earth messengers' who don't wear shoes, because of the role we play here. However, it's not all the time. You'll see as you start playing the game," he concluded.

Every comment just led to a million more questions, and I sighed, "What game?"

"It's just known as 'the game' and people come here from all over the world, and even interdimensionally, as you did, to play it. Participants enter with a question they want to answer, big life questions they may have been trying to resolve for a long time. The electromagnetic field of each entrant is scanned before beginning the game to determine the level of play they are ready for. The intention is that everyone succeeds, so clues are geared accordingly. All members of the community are involved in the game and it is the basis of our economy and also shapes the social offerings you will find here," he explained cursorily.

"**Here**?" I said, looking at the open expanse around me and puzzled by what community and social offerings he was referring to.

"No… in the community where I will take you now. It's called Escalante de Luz, which means 'climber of light.'"

"You also said the game is the basis of the economy, which I assume means you use a form of money. Whatever your medium of exchange, I know I don't have any," I interjected, wondering if this meant I was going to be sent back through the wormhole.

41

"Don't worry," Trevor assured me. "It's a little complicated, but basically anyone who comes to play the game, either interdimensionally or not, has the means to participate, or is provided for. Money is never a determining factor in who can play the game. It is more a matter of readiness. I know it's a lot to absorb. It's a good thing you are a fast learner."

I looked back down at what I was wearing and asked, "Is this what all the females wear here?"

"No," he said chuckling. "I'm not sure what you are imagining about the community, but everyone is very individual in their expression. This is just something comfortable until we get to the community, where you can choose something to your liking. It also has filaments of monoatomic gold and platinum for helping you to integrate the new frequencies."

"I must admit it does feel really good," I replied, excited by what was coming next.

Trevor pulled a device resembling a smart phone from a pouch he had hanging from his belt and simply spoke to it saying, "Transport vehicle uncloak and activate."

Then to my amazement, something resembling what I think of as a saucer-shaped UFO appeared, but relatively small… perhaps the sports car version. The chassis alloys weren't like anything I had ever seen before. It didn't appear to be metal, but was more like the dynamic energy of the plasma field I had come through with patterns of light and color that changed depending on… what?… what was it I was picking up?

Feeling a little foolish, I blurted out, "Is this like some kind of giant mood ring?"

Trevor looked at me surprised that I was perceiving so well, so quickly. "There is an element of that, but it is also much more, as you will see when we get in."

"Whoa, this is amazing. We are definitely not in my time-space reality," I said. "What year is it on the planet?"

"In linear time it is the year 2052."

"Was this ship or vehicle, or whatever you call this, sitting here the whole time I've been here?" I said, noticing that it was placed in between the thermal pool I had been in and where Trevor was sitting.

"Yes."

"How did I avoid running into it when I came over to talk to you?"

"You actually veered from walking a straight line to where I was because you sensed it. It's when you were picking up the information through your feet and getting overloaded with the geometric patterns, which you didn't know how to interpret. The **knowing** beyond your intellect was guiding you. It has a lot to do with trusting what you feel. Anyway, shall we?" he said as he motioned toward the craft.

"Sure," I said, a little perplexed about how to do that.

Trevor then spoke into the smart phone, "ramp down," and a ramp extended from the lower portion of the vehicle, as a panel raised to give us access.

The ship was spacious inside and there were two connected seats in the center of the vehicle that looked like futuristic La-Z-boy recliners. Trevor took one of the seats and invited me to take the other. As soon as I was seated he said, "viewing area, **please**," and the chairs raised to the navigation deck, as if on some type of hydraulic lift.

I had a momentary memory flash of someone I knew politely talking to her vehicle as if it was alive, but the impression was gone before I could place it.

"You can give the vehicle the name of the place you want to go, just as you would with a GPS from your dimension, and you can sit back and enjoy the trip without having to think about it. Or, you can operate it manually, which basically means being more interactive with what you encounter along the way," Trevor suggested.

"Why would I want to operate it manually, if I could basically just check out and let it take me where I tell it to go?"

"Because it's fun. I'll show you," he said. "We're going to re-cloak before we take off though, because we are in a conservation area. We only uncloak when we get into populated areas, to make landing easier."

"So how many of these vehicles are out there and how do you avoid crashing into each other, if you are cloaked?" I wondered out loud.

Trevor dutifully explained, "There actually aren't as many of these vehicles as you might think. There are teleportation devices that most people use for getting between routine spaces almost instantly. This kind of transport vehicle is more for leisurely sightseeing. I thought it would feel less disorienting to you and be more enjoyable. Believe it or not, people also actually delight in walking both on paths within the community and to outlying nature areas.

As far as avoiding collisions, there are sensing devices as a part of the GPS system, when we are on automatic, and we use our own sensing capacities when we are operating manually, just like when you sensed the cloaked vehicle on the ground. It definitely has an energy field that can be felt when you are in close proximity to it. We just agree to cloak because we prefer having a visually uncluttered landscape in the conservation areas."

"Okay, let's get going," Trevor said as he instructed the craft, "manual system engage" and it began to lift off the ground.

"Wait a second," I said, "I don't see any controls."

"I am the controls," said Trevor. "This vehicle is thought responsive and when I am sitting in the driver's seat it is syncing to my neural network and becomes an extension of me. You made the mood ring analogy and I said that was a part of what is happening. So, basically, the color patterns in the body of the vehicle change to reflect the mood of the operator. It is just another way of seeing what's going on with us in everything around us. Of course, when we're cloaked others don't see it."

"So what's the power source?" I asked, surprising myself with the question, because I didn't remember having any strong scientific inclinations. But, this stuff... this place... was fascinating in a way that made me want to know more.

"Well, I can see you are going to keep me on my toes," Trevor said, with the appreciation of a teacher whose students are eager to learn. "It's a magnetic plasma fusion containment engine. It's like tapping the power of a chunk of the sun that's contained in a magnetic bottle. It creates very rapid propulsion, when needed, but we can adjust our speed at will."

As we rose out of the canyon to make our way to Escalante de Luz, the overview of the seemingly endless expanse was breathtaking. The stage was perfectly lit as the sun brushed the cliff walls with a saturation of reds with hints of gold that removed any doubt of divine presence.

Trevor continued with the geography lesson, "As I said before, we're in the region known as the Escalante. This particular part of it is called the Grand Staircase. The geological formations here span eons of time. The terrain and the remoteness made it difficult to create the infrastructure needed to support residential developments, the way they were done at the beginning of the twenty-first century. Human endeavors have always been limited on these lands, yet the isolation has and continues to attract seekers of adventure or solitude, and those who hope to come into closer relationship with the natural world."

Progressing further away from the conservation area, I noticed what seemed to be a flock of birds. They were so thick they appeared to be a dark cloud, but what amazed me most was the way they were flying. En masse they would rapidly change course, creating different shapes, like they were telling a story in the sky with different scenes and characters. I was entranced.

Trevor glanced over at me, and from the look of astonishment on my face he commented, "I take it you've never seen that before. It's a flock of starlings in murmuration. Pretty incredible, isn't it?"

"Ya, how do they do that... I mean turn on a dime in perfect synchronicity without crashing into each other?"

"Well, for one thing animals aren't preoccupied with a million thoughts, like humans are. They are present to the moment. In the case of murmuration, which is also common with schools of fish, they have synced so precisely to each other's energy fields that they are literally functioning as one mind."

Trevor began to accelerate the transport vehicle in the direction of the flock of birds and said, "Let's have some fun!"

I screamed, "What are you doing? You are going to run right into them and hurt them!!!"

"No, I'm not," Trevor assured calmly, "We are going to mind-meld. Breathe and tune to them."

By this point we had closed in on the flock and caught the edge of their wave. Trevor was totally silent and by the calm in his body and the look in his eyes I could tell he was functioning outside of himself, feeling and riding the shifting flow. I let go of my momentary angst and dropped into breath and awareness as I became a part of the most incredible dance I could ever imagine. The high of it, as we soared, dove, exploded out and collapsed back in, all in perfect rhythm with a collective intelligence, was beyond words.

When Trevor finally separated off from the flock, he said, "See the advantage of flying manually?"

All I could say was, "Oh, my God!"

CHAPTER 6

Escalante de Luz

As we left the Grand Staircase to head back to Escalante de Luz, Trevor felt my need for silence in order to savor the overwhelming richness of the unexpected feast I found myself at.

We were probably twenty miles out from the community when we began to pass what I presumed were housing and commercial developments. While each one varied in architectural style they all had a sense of circularity and flow, more than square grid patterns. There were no billboards, strip malls or giant box stores claiming dominance in the landscape, instead I saw gardens growing food, interspersed between clusters of small dwelling spaces.

"Are there shopping centers here?" I finally asked, giving Trevor permission to respond to my thoughts.

"Those are mixed-use areas you are seeing. The feel of it is more like the old villages in Europe where trades and needs intertwined and felt like an integrated whole. We don't consume that much here and there is an emphasis on creative expression, which includes things like textiles, ceramics, and woodworking. You will see the shared workspaces in the community core center when we get there. Each of the cluster communities has a core center that is really the hub of activity and social engagement. That's why the living spaces are relatively small. They are simply for personal renewal and introspection. The inner longing people from your time sought to fill up with stuff, we satisfy with creative collaboration and play."

"I think Buckminster Fuller would have liked it here," I reflected, thinking about a quote I had once heard by him. "He said that whenever he was working on a problem, he never thought about beauty, but when he arrived at a solution, if it wasn't beautiful he knew it was wrong."

"Buckminster Fuller did enjoy his visit here," Trevor said nonchalantly.

"What?... Get out of here... you are messing with me now, aren't you?" I said as I reached over and playfully pushed Trevor on the shoulder, like a big brother I never had. I was surprised by how quickly I was coming to like him and feel comfortable being with him.

"Well, actually, no I'm not messing with you," Trevor said, appreciating the peculiar expression as a gesture of fondness and familiarity. "Most people don't know that a midlife crisis in 1927 left 'Bucky' on the verge of suicide.

He felt he had completely failed at everything in his life, and in that void he accessed a larger part of himself, which brought him into alignment with this **future** vision of what is possible. It was after his time here that he returned and stated his intent to turn his life into 'an experiment to find what a single individual can contribute to changing the world and benefiting all humanity.'"

"Wow, something just occurred to me," I said, the wheels of my mind spinning with excitement. "So, you're telling me that Buckminster Fuller was here in 1927, but he was experiencing what I am experiencing in 2052 as a **future** vision and then he **went back** and incorporated that into his life from there forward; which would mean that he visited the future in order to help create it."

"Yes, you could say that, but remember that it is actually all happening simultaneously. One more refinement is that he didn't bring his body with him, the way you did."

"Okay, help me out on that one," I said, wondering if my brain circuits were going to overload and start shooting sparks out of my ears.

"Well, most of you identify with your body as who you are, but actually the essence of you transcends the body. It would be like thinking the suitcase you have your belongings packed in is you. No one ever talks about their suitcase having taken a trip, as if that was them. You experienced it when you entered the coma and were aware of everything going on around you, even things happening at a distance. If you were just the body, that wouldn't have been possible."

"So, basically you're saying that Buckminster Fuller came without a suitcase." I did a little low toned humpf in my throat to indicate curious consideration.

My attention turned toward the smattering of other transport vehicles that began turning on their lights and looked like magical fireflies hovering around the exquisite adobe Mothership welcoming us home for the evening.

"Man, this is a trip!" I said.

"Which part of it is **a trip**? The center, the simultaneity, the true nature of your being…?" Trevor inquired for clarity.

"All of it!"

Trevor gave a little nod of affirmation, as he glanced over at me, not expecting me to engage in the gaze, because I was literally lost in a foreign world.

"This reality is always a lot to process for the interdimensionals, however, those of you who find your way here are generally cut from a different cloth and, to some extent, being here will quickly feel like coming home."

The phrase "cut from a different cloth" shot through me and my heart registered a sweet sadness as I looked at Trevor.

"Chris, your official registration for the game will be tomorrow, but you seem like one of those people who are twitching to get off the starting block. So, I would say that unofficially you are already in the game."

"Did I break some rule?"

"No, there really are no rules and you aren't competing against anyone else. The main thing will be to think about the question you want to find an answer to and then relax and enjoy yourself as you sleuth your way through the information that is coming to you." Trevor said, as he gently guided the transport vehicle into a holding bay.

"Okay, my friend, why don't you hop out and I'll take you to both the textile and the re-use trading pods so you can pick out some clothes you would like to wear," Trevor said as he opened the access hatch and extended the ramp.

"I was going to give you a quick tour of the center too, but I think just getting you situated in your room with whatever you will need for tonight will have filled you to capacity for today."

"I keep thinking I'm going to wake up and this lovely little dream will be over," I confessed.

"Well, I suppose that is a possible scenario, isn't it. One dream is as good as the next." He said, seemingly presenting me with some kind of cryptic riddle. "It's really all up to you."

The air was particularly still and perfectly warm, as we exited the holding bay to pick up the multicolored, mosaic tile pathway into the center, which was still dimly visible in the fading light. The smooth tiles felt good against my bare feet and I was appreciating that their upgraded sensing capacity was giving me time to get up to speed with where I had arrived before inundating me with too much information.

It is only about fifty yards to the center entrance and I can see a lively scene inside with people moving between the various pods, and stopping to connect with each other along the way. It has the feel of people milling about at a party. I can also see people occupying little nooks, either as couples in intimate conversation, or alone reading. Even though Trevor said the year is 2052, the clothing styles could just as easily be from my time-space reality, but then I come from Berkeley where the range of personal expression in clothing is not the norm. What strikes me as different here is the percentage of people in the community who are obviously of blended race, and how gorgeous those combinations are to me. Although there are a range of body shapes and sizes, the overall commonality is vibrancy.

Children are laughing and playing, both inside the complex and in the courtyard, with a variety of sculpted mythical creatures… dragons… unicorns… wizards… giants and other somewhat menacing looking beings. What strikes me as unusual is that none of the characters being played by the children are attempting to conquer or slay the beasts, or each other for that matter. Instead, they are talking about taking on the powers of the creature they are engaging with in order to succeed at the missions they are on.

Entering the community core center, my eyes went first to the central atrium, which is probably about the size of a gymnasium… large enough anyway to house a handful of ornate, wrought iron benches interspersed between garden and water features. An array of colorful butterflies flitted about the garden, finding their way to branches to tuck themselves in for the night. Everything about the complex feels like ease, reverence, beauty and flow. Interior cob walls become part of the art, flowing into alcoves with altars displaying objects as odes to the Earth… feathers, bones, shells, stones… both unaltered and embellished. Stained glass skylights depict nature and mesmerizing geometric patterns. Ceiling tract lighting is full-spectrum, warm and soothing, unlike the harsh lighting I am familiar with in public buildings.

Trevor gently took my elbow to guide me to where I could find some clothing, knowing that unless he kept me moving it could take a long time to get there.

"We'll do the full tour tomorrow," he said, "…I promise."

For a moment I wondered what people passing us must think about this dazed looking, barefoot young woman with nothing but a simple shift on and no bra or underwear. While it isn't see-through, it definitely could be considered suggestive by the way it lays close to my fully developed figure. Yet, no one seemed to think anything of it, or at least I wasn't picking up on being sexually checked out the way I was accustomed to. People all just smiled at us and some had a few warm words of greeting for Trevor.

"There are two possibilities for clothing," Trevor started to explain. "You've probably already noticed that there are a variety of pods that branch off from the hub of the center. They each have different purposes and, as I mentioned earlier, they serve as collective, creative studios. The one I am thinking of is the textile pod and there is also more of a store, which is called the re-use trading pod. People design and make their own clothing in the textile pod. Sometimes there are items that people have made just because they love working with textiles, but they don't want to add them to their wardrobe, so they leave them for someone else to select. The items at the re-use trading pod are pieces that have been put back into circulation after someone feels complete with enjoying them and they want to try something new."

"We would call that a thrift store." I said, feeling like I recognized **something** as familiar.

"So, do you have a sense of which one you want to check out first?" Trevor asked.

"Ya, I think the re-use trading pod. I love shopping at thrift stores, and they probably have better prices," I said, thinking in terms of what I had known.

I was also surprised that Trevor was up for shopping with me. At first I thought he might find a girl my age in the community to go with me. Then I realized that I don't have any way to pay for it and I couldn't imagine Trevor wanting to unleash two teenage girls with some type of credit card.

Picking up on my thought he said, "We will pay with my TD, or Transaction Device. It's this thing you saw me use to start the transport vehicle," he indicated as he turned his hip to me and pointed to the smart phone looking device in the pouch on his belt. "You will be issued one when I take you to get registered for the game tomorrow. You will be shown how all the features work then. Anyway, we're here at the re-use trading pod now, so let's go in and have a look."

The motion-sensitive glass doors slid back as we approached and we walked in. I wasn't sure I would find anything I liked here, but there are actually a ton of really cool and unique options for putting something together. Trevor noticed how thrift store treasure hunting had given me a second wind and he was quick to point out, "remember you just need some things to get you through the next couple of days. You can come back at your leisure and get creative with combining things."

I chuckled to myself, realizing that some things never change and that shopping was really a conciliatory act on Trevor's part.

They had a really awesome selection of cowboy boots. I had always dreamed of getting some and I scored a rose red pair that fit just right, with brown and ivory detailing that looked like flames. Then I found a dusty rose, short sleeved, high-low t-shirt knit top with a large slit down each arm. To complete it I spotted some destroyed denim shorts. I also grabbed a pair of stargazer, tie-dyed leggings, since I don't yet know what to expect temperature-wise in the next few days. A beautiful abalone shell comb caught my eye, which I could use to pull my long black hair back on one side to create an asymmetrical style with my bangs draping over my brow on the other side. I picked it up as well.

"Do you want anything to sleep in?" Trevor asked.

I looked down at what I was wearing and said, "actually, this is really comfortable. Can I sleep in this?"

"Sure."

The article of clothing I had on reminded me that it would be good to get some underclothing, but I didn't figure they had that at the re-use store and I was embarrassed to mention it to Trevor. Fortunately the people here are good at reading thoughts and the young woman assisting in the shop stepped from behind the desk and approached me. Trevor picked up that he should turn and look at something else to make it more comfortable for me to talk to her.

The petite young blond woman, in a 1930s cadet dress that would bring anyone's eyes to attention, warmly asked, "Is this your first time here?"

I'm sure she could tell from what I was wearing that I was a new arrival and her respectful inquiry put me at ease. I let her navigate the conversation to spare me feeling awkward.

"Yes," was all I said.

"Let me show you around then, since not everything we carry is re-used," she said matter-of-factly, as she guided me to the lingerie section in the back near the dressing rooms.

Before we got too far away, Trevor cleared his throat and the clerk turned around. "Here," he said, handing her his TD, "just put everything on there when she is finished."

"Thanks, Trevor," she said with a tender familiarity.

She turned around and came back down the aisle to where I was standing and we continued to the back of the store. I wanted to ask her if she knew Trevor, but I didn't. I also noticed I was feeling a sense of connection to him already and deep appreciation for the kindness he was showing me.

After picking the few things that I needed, I handed them to the really sweet clerk and she completed the transaction. She started placing them in a bag, which was neither plastic nor paper, but some thin, sturdy fiber.

"You can leave the boots and a pair of socks out and I'll wear those," I said and she passed them over the counter. I slipped them on and looked down at the combination. I love the way cowboy boots can make anything you're wearing look really cool, I thought to myself.

"I like your choices," she said cheerfully. "Maybe I'll see you here again?"

"Yes, I hope so," I said as I turned to rejoin Trevor.

"Oh wait," she said, handing me the TD, "please give this back to Trevor."

We left the re-use trading pod and walked out onto a cobble stone path headed in the opposite direction of where we had come in. The community center is like a wagon wheel with paths that branch from its center out to an array of special use pods. Those walkways all have various types of coverings, but the paths beyond the center, like the one we are on now, are open to the incredible night sky. I had only seen night skies through the ambient light of a city and as I took in the enormity of the sky and the density of endless galaxies before me, I realized that my experience had been limited.

"Where are we going now?" I asked Trevor, feeling like wherever it was it would be amazing.

"I'm taking you to the guest facilities just ahead. It's an easy walk, but if you are carrying a lot of things sometime, there are little hover crafts, sort of like what you would think of as a golf cart, which you can catch back to the center."

The path took us past the edge of a peach orchard in full bloom, the fragrance of it still lingering in the night air. I could see the guest facilities ahead, but they looked more like demonstration architectural sites than what I think of as short-term housing units. Multistoried, rectangular boxes are what come to mind in association with motels or hotels. Here there are a variety of shapes, little cob hobbit houses, yurts, geodesic domes, and even some large Earthships resembling creatures you might meet at a *Starwars* outpost bar, which appear to have multiple guestrooms. There is even a restored VW Westfalia, probably for the interdimensionals from the 1960s.

"I know it's not that late yet, but given how much new information you have had to process today, I thought you might want some downtime. Being alone will also give you a chance to think about the question you want to begin the game with tomorrow," Trevor offered just as we arrived at one of the Earthships.

The light metal alloy panels retracted into the arched doorway as we approached. He gestured for me to head to the right when we were inside. "Your room is this way. It's small, but I think you will find everything you need."

When we reached my room, he passed his hand over the red light to the side of the door and we entered. He gave me a second to generally look around and orient and then directed my attention to each of the features I might have trouble figuring out. The interior cob walls were painted mauve with turquoise tile inlays on the hearth of the rounded fireplace in the corner. A red, gold, and purple weaving graced the wall and the wood floor was open with a basket of yoga mats, meditation cushions and such next to a small, antique black oak writing desk. On the other wall was a traditional Mexican Equipale loveseat with a curved pigskin back and bench supported by cross-hatched cedar strips below. Above it was a small inset bookshelf with a few books and other knick knacks they probably had there more for style than as something people really still read. In general, it seemed out of context with the technology of the time. However, these rooms might be set up to give the interdimensionals a sense of familiar comfort. There was one other room… the bathroom with a recognizable toilet and shower. Some things never change, thank God. What I didn't see was a closet or a bed.

"You people still have to sleep, don't you?" I asked a little nervously.

"Oh, yes," Trevor said. "By all means, let me show you the bed."

He pressed a button on the wall control panel and the two wooden support beams across the ceiling, which were carved in the shape of whales, began lowering. I could see it was the frame of a sleeping platform. As I looked up into the opening created by the lowered platform, I could see a clear dome that offered optimal night sky viewing. There was sufficient space in the room to walk around the lowered bed, but not much more. The bedding look absolutely cushy, with an abundance of pillows and a fluffy comforter out of something like down or wool.

"You can either leave the bed on this level and sleep next to the fire, or you can use this remote control to raise it back into the ceiling after you get in. It makes a perfect, cozy nest for stargazing and, if you want to layer your sensory experience, you can listen to binaural beats to balance your brain at the same time. You can, of course, listen to anything else of your own choosing as well. The dome is wired for sound and, if you want, you can make it into a sensurround theater by pressing this control and a screen will cover the inside of the dome," he said, as he demonstrated with the controller. "You can use the TD you will receive tomorrow to make some music and video selections."

"There is a closet and storage area through this side door," he said as we walked into the bathroom and he opened the closet door to give me a quick peek. There are also some basic toiletries here in the cabinet, which will hopefully meet your needs," he gestured. "The toilets are an advanced composting design that use ultraviolet and blue light in specific frequency ranges to eliminate pathogens. The waste is then flushed into the solar sewage walls around the community for further filtering and purification—the end result being pure water and beautiful new topsoil."

"When you say sewage walls, you mean those things that look like greenhouses?" I asked.

"Well, yes, they actually are greenhouses," he continued, trying to quickly move on to the remaining basics so we could each have some evening left to renew. "The shower should be pretty straight forward and this is a one person infrared sauna," he concluded, pointing to the wooden enclosure next to the shower.

"One last question," I said, "Is there anywhere I can get a little bit of food?"

"Oh, God, I apologize," Trevor said sheepishly. "There is so much to cover to get people integrated here that I sometimes forget that people just showing up here still need to eat regularly."

"You mean you don't?" I said in amazement.

"It's more of a social and sensory treat than a necessity," he admitted. "We can talk more about that tomorrow. In the meantime, you should be able to find some high-energy offerings here to take care of you for tonight," he said, as he revealed yet another hidden compartment in the wall. It was like a mini automat vending machine with sandwiches, superfood juices, salads, nuts and energy bars.

"Well, I guess my fantasy about a standard concession stand to go with the sensurround theater is out," I said only half-jokingly.

"Ah yes, well I suppose all fantasies can be fulfilled one way or another here. Just give us time. I'll come pick you up tomorrow at 8:00 am to give you the full tour of the community and to get you registered. Is there anything else you need tonight?"

"Are there any alarm clocks here so I will be ready on time?"

"Yes, I already preset one for you next to the bed so you wouldn't have to figure it out. When it goes off, just tell it to stop and it will. If something comes up that you need help with, just press the assistance button on the control panel on the wall and speak. See you tomorrow then?"

"Yes, thank you. Sleep well, Trevor."

"You too, Chris."

He left and I noticed how odd it felt to be alone in such a foreign place and to be so at peace with it. Although the sense of being alone, as I had known it, had very quickly lost its meaning. Maybe I didn't want to answer my question in the game, if it meant I would have to leave here.

CHAPTER 7

Orientation to the Game

The expected 8:00 am knock on the door came and I jumped from the loveseat, excited for the next part of the adventure Trevor was going to take me on. I pressed the button on the control panel to retract the door only to find a short, redheaded woman I guessed to be in her 50s. Although the stylish bob framing her elf-like face and the sparkling blue eyes lent a sense of mischief and awestruck wonder to her, she wasn't Trevor.

"Uh, hi," I said wondering if she was a neighboring guest resident who needed something.

"Hi, Chris, I'm Joelle. Trevor asked me if I could give you a tour of the center this morning and then get you over to the welcome center to register for the game," she said enthusiastically.

"Oh, okay," I said, with disappointment in my voice.

"Trevor sends his apologies. There was an unexpected arrival of an interdimensional in the canyon and he had to dash off," Joelle explained.

"Is that his job?" I asked.

"It's what he loves doing as the major part of his contribution to the game."

"Does everyone in the community participate in the game?" I asked, trying to remember if Trevor had already told me that as part of the download I had gotten yesterday.

"Yes, our community has become sort of a tourist destination for people who are at a transition point in their lives and who want to **play** with new ideas and see possibilities reflected from a fresh perspective. When people are in the mode of playing they are more willing to disband disbelief and be in an imaginative flow."

Joelle could see that I was trying to understand how all of this works on a practical level and she continued, "If you're ready to go, we can talk while we walk."

"Ya, sure. I'm ready," I said feeling a little naked going out for the day without a backpack, cell, or any of the various and sundry items I was accustomed to carrying.

"The game isn't all that we do here, but it is a part of a creative focus we really enjoy. You'll see on the tour the different ways that gets expressed. For example, I manage the wellness center, which is a combination of subtle energy technologies, optimal nutrition and fitness programs. There are also a variety of holistic practitioners who have adjoining treatment spaces. I'll point that out as a part of our whirlwind tour of the center. If you want, you can come and have a balancing session when you have some downtime."

"I don't know that much about that type of thing, but it sounds pretty cool and based on how healthy you all look, you must be doing something right," I said, noticing that I was having a little trouble keeping up with Joelle's springy step.

We were approaching the outer ring of pods off the main building. At this early hour, the sun was already feeling wonderfully warm on my skin. I had been focused on the path and the conversation and when I finally really looked up, I was blown away by the desert, rich with spring bloom. Why hadn't I noticed this overwhelming beauty before? Perhaps it's the fresh angle on things that morning light brings, as it draws the richness of a place to the forefront for those not yet jarred from their stillness or clad with the blinders of preoccupation.

Joelle paused and respectfully let me have my moment of awe before adding commentary of her own. "The softness of the morning light makes the colors of everything more pronounced. Also, some of the plants close their blossoms in the heat of the day. It is magnificent, isn't it?"

When it felt right to continue walking, Joelle began identifying the different pods and features of the community center that we could see from this vantage point. "Right ahead of us is the re-use trading store," she said.

I recognized it from last night, although things always look different from the opposite angle and in the daylight.

"To the left of that is the textile center, with every type of textile supply and equipment you can imagine. Many of the pods, like that one, are shared workspaces. To the left of the textile pod is the woodworking pod, to the left of that the metal shop, to the left of that the ceramics and fine arts studios. I'll point out the pods that continue around to the other side when we go into the community center. From where we are now you can also see the general store, which carries local artisans' goods and basic needs. It also has a commercial kitchen attached for food related classes and preparation of community dinners that are part of seasonal celebrations. To the right of the general store is the Rawsome Café, which has wonderful soups, salads, sandwiches, and fresh juices all made on site, with much of the produce from the organic gardens between there and the fruit and nut orchards you probably passed last night."

"Yes, we did pass them and the fragrance was intoxicating, but before we get off the subject of food, does the café have any Middle Eastern items on the menu?"

"The menu changes and people put in special requests for theme evenings. So, the answer to your question would be, yes."

Joelle and I approached one of the main doors to the center, which slid open automatically and we went in. I thought that the center might be quieter during the day, anticipating that people would be at jobs working, but the hum of this hub seemed to be from sunrise to well past dark. The butterflies in the central atrium were now fully active and it was a place I knew I wanted to come back to and just hang for a while.

"Joelle, this might sound like a dumb question, but I don't really feel like being called Chris here, and it occurred to me when I saw all the butterflies last night that it would be really cool to change my name to Chrysalis. Is it possible to do that since I am sort of making a fresh start?"

"I don't see why not," Joelle responded. "When you get your TD it will be calibrated to you based on your energy field, or individual frequency, so the names we use are for social purposes more than official identification."

"Awesome!"

"Let's go around the atrium to the other side so I can point out the pods we couldn't see from outside. The first pod to the right of the main entrance is the welcome center and the administration office.

We'll come back to that to get you registered for the game, although they already know you're here. Next to that is a business center with shared equipment and workspaces. The telecommunication center is also there for dealing with TD issues. As you've seen the personal living spaces are quite modest, and a lot of what you would call work is done in shared spaces here at the center. Next to that is a communication center with recording, broadcasting and filmmaking equipment, for those who like to play in that realm," Joelle said as we breezed past each of them, with only the thumbnail details.

She continued, "You'll notice that the pods are staggered, to provide ample space for each, while maintaining a sense of connection and flow. They are also grouped by function, which will help you remember where things are. So food, clothing and consumables are together. There is the artisan workshop section, the business and communication section, the education section, health and healing, and the large performance hall directly across from the main entrance.

A quick, easy way to find things will be with the GPS on your TD, and a fun way to identify them is by their individual paths that tie into their purpose. We are coming up to some of my favorite examples of that. So, looking at the path out to the next pod, what would you guess it to be?" Joelle queried as she paused to give me time to look at it and take in the details.

There was a relatively short walkway of cobbled stone, with carved marble pillars in the shape of upstretched arms holding open books that linked together to form a covering for the path.

"Something to do with learning?" I said, wondering if I was already receiving training for the game.

"Yes, good!" Joelle affirmed, "It is the intergenerational learning center, which is our education system, although we don't define our learning population as only children and young adults. Rather, we consider learning to be a lifelong process. Because of the rapid advances in technology, the younger generations are often more knowledgeable in that area. So, sometimes the elders are in the teaching role and sometimes the youth are. I think you will find it interesting."

I'm sure I will, I thought and Joelle smiled in response.

"Do you see the path that branches off from the intergenerational learning center?" Joelle continued with her brainteasers.

"A little bit," I said, knowing that I was probably missing important details.

"Let's walk out there for a second."

We walked out the path to the intergenerational learning center and then took the branch that led to the next mystery pod. I could see little, deep blue resin chips randomly embedded in swirling patterns. They looked like fingernail-sized solar collectors and I noticed this path was uncovered, which would make sense with the collectors. I could also tell from the shape of the pod that the roof was retractable, but what really caught my eye was the antique armillary sphere sitting on a marble pedestal between the end of the path and the entrance to the building. I gasped and my brow furrowed as I tried to register the association with the brass object the sun was glinting off of.

"Are you okay?" Joelle asked.

"Ya, just some sort of déjà vu with this path." I cleared my throat and did a little shake of my head to bring myself back to the question about the purpose of the building, as indicated by the walkway.

"I'm thinking that at night these little chips light up and look like a starscape. The building also seems to have something to do with astronomy."

"Again, excellent," Joelle congratulated me. "It is an observatory and also a collective dream space. Another bit of information about it you might find interesting is that this is photocatalytic concrete," she said, pointing to the substrate material in the walkway.

"Okay, so what's unique about it?"

"The photocatalysts in the concrete accelerate chemical reactions, whereby strong sunlight or ultraviolet light decomposes organic materials in a slow, natural process. Dirt, soot, mold, bacteria and chemicals that cause odors are among the many substances they decompose. In other words, it handles a lot of pollutants."

"Wow, it's good to know that all of these things finally got figured out," I reflected appreciatively.

"Actually, most of what you will find here in terms of technology isn't that far off from what exists, at least in prototype, in your dimension. The main difference here is the realization that no technology can change the course of humanity without a healthy relationship with the Earth and each other."

"So in other words it was a shift from head to heart that made this possible," I clarified before losing sight of the important point she was making.

"Yes, and that's why we are excited to host people from your dimension... so that you can see that this is really not that out of reach," she added and paused.

"I feel like I'm dreaming. All I ever heard was that this type of 'utopian' reality could never happen because it goes against human nature," I reflected.

"The human mind wants to make everything very simple... black and white... and really it's all a paradox. Your prior experience was an aspect of human nature, but so is this. It would be like saying that a baby will never go beyond crawling because that is its nature, when in fact it is only one phase of its development. Thank God babies aren't able to talk themselves out of the potential they sense within.

What we bring to the forefront is a choice. I would also say that what was generally agreed upon in your time was based on mistaken identity. These are big questions and you have just begun... Shall we continue?"

"Sure," I said, bringing my attention back to the features of the community.

"A few more important pods to point out and then we will loop back to the welcome center," Joelle said, still full of energy. "Most important is the wellness center, of course, since that's **my** baby! Off of the wellness center there are rejuvenation rooms with private hot tubs that look out onto ornamental gardens."

I could see that we were about back to where we started and Joelle concluded the tour with, "Last but not least, the performance hall, which is used for plays, concerts, yoga and dance classes, and community celebrations like wedding receptions, or any type of large gathering. The immersions also happen here, which you will find out about."

She stopped as if the race was now over and took a big breath and then sighed, "Okay, so let's get you over to the welcome center to get your TD and to have your question for the game officially entered. Then you'll be off and running on your own."

The idea of that seemed a little overwhelming, but also exciting, in what seems a very safe and friendly environment. When we reached the welcome center, I discovered I was already signed up for a group orientation to "the game" at 10:30. Joelle introduced me to the program director to make sure there was no problem with the name change.

"Max, this is Chrysalis, but I think you probably show her on the orientation roll as Chris."

"Hmm, that's funny. We have the name as Chris with a question mark after it. I guess there was an identity question already noted. Anyway, nice to meet you Chrysalis," Max said chirpily, as he extended his thick hand and shook mine vigorously.

Max looked Latino and was average height with a stocky, muscular build that made him look more like a high school wrestling coach than a game administrator. I don't know, maybe it was all the raw food and clean air that had these people acting way more like energizer bunnies than I was used to, but not frenetic ones. It felt good, but foreign, which made me think that my "upgrade" to this dimension hadn't yet fully kicked in.

"Okay, Chrysalis, it was great to meet you!" Joelle said as she gave my elbow a squeeze. "I have to get over to open the wellness center now, but I hope you will come check it out soon."

"Yes, I'm really curious about how all of that works here. Thanks for taking me around this morning."

Next thing I knew Max was guiding me into the registration office where four other people, all around my age, were getting signed in.

"Could I have your attention, please?" Max announced. "When I call your name will you please go to the scanning booth to my right so we can calibrate your TDs to you. Don't worry about how they function. I will go over that with you in the orientation. As we do the voice scan, you will also state your question for the game."

I could tell by the similarly dazed looks on the faces of everyone in the orientation group that they were probably interdimensionals as well. I also get the sense we are all from the same time-space reality.

As Max went down the list and called each name, I thought I would make a game out of it by making up a little story in my mind about each of them.

"Cali," Max called.

Her name could be a pet name for "California," since she looks like a typical California blond, bronzed girl. She has a hip vibe, like maybe she is a snowboarder just back from the Olympics. Her parents are divorced and she lives with her mother who is devoted to the grueling routine of a competitive athlete. She is a bit older than the rest of the group.

"Chrysalis," Max announced, but it took me a moment to register because I had only heard it spoken twice now, and I was still getting used to it. I disengaged my mind from the fictitious story project and composed myself, as I made my way to the scanning booth.

"Hi, Chrysalis," the lovely woman at the booth said in almost a whisper. "Can you tell me what the question is you want to answer in the game?"

"Umm," I hesitated slightly, "I guess I want to know why I'm here."

Before I could go on, the woman operating the equipment said, "I need you to speak directly into the microphone because it is recording your voice signature, and you don't need to whisper just because I was speaking softly. Just speak normally."

"Okay," I said, feeling a little self-conscious. "The question I would like an answer to is, Why am I here? I don't really mean **here**, but in the dimension I came from. It feels like I'm not finished there and I want to know why."

The woman smiled without commentary on my question, "Thank you, Chrysalis. It will take a few minutes to have your TD calibrated.

We will pass them all out when the orientation begins. You can go back to your seat now."

I walked back to my seat, still mulling over the question in my mind, and the names that followed on the roll call became a blur. I guess they would just have to remain storyless for now.

"Kai," Max continued down the list, "Luna, Sage, Zander... is Zander here yet?" Max repeated.

"Saphira," Max said to the woman working the scanning device. "Is Zander the unexpected arrival who Trevor is out retrieving?"

"Yes," Saphira said. "They should be arriving momentarily."

Just as she said that, Trevor hurriedly made his way into the room with Zander, a particularly disoriented looking arrival. I was feeling empathy for the poor guy having to take in so much so quickly. It would be enough to make any person's head spin.

"Trevor, will you show Zander over to the scanning area?" Max requested, not wanting to throw this guy into the mix on his own any sooner than necessary.

I was sitting close enough to the scanning equipment that I heard Trevor say to Zander, "I'm sure you have a million questions about where you are and why you are here, but do you also have a question about the dimension you just came from?"

Zander, a sheepish looking, tall white kid with a little of something else mixed in, because he has a moon-shaped flat face with slightly almond shaped brown eyes, asked, "Will I make it through high school?"

I picked up a vibe of high-functioning autism and having been bullied. I also noticed that he was wearing loose fitting pants and a long, sleeveless tank top in the same fabric of the dress I was given when I arrived. The outfit looked like a cross between pajamas and the polyester athletic pants the homies would wear to play hoops on the street.

It felt good to know, that at least in the time he would be here to play the game, he would be safe and I wanted to be a part of making him feel supported. Trevor picked up on my willingness to help Zander get oriented and signaled for me to come over.

"Hey, Chris," Trevor began, and I interrupted before he went on.

"Actually, as of this morning, I'm calling myself Chrysalis," I said, apologetic for having interrupted.

"Awesome," Trevor said. "I can see how that suits you better. Anyway, Chrysalis, Zander can use some extra support in getting comfortable with this place. I'm kind of sensing you might be up for that, which would really be appreciated because I need to be somewhere else."

"Absolutely, no problem," I said with a sense of pride that Trevor felt he could rely on me.

"Great! I hope to catch both of you later. Have a wonderful day and welcome!" he said as he darted out the door in the direction of the transportation vehicle hangar.

With the process of registering our questions complete, Max guided us over to a classroom in the intergenerational learning center for the orientation on how to use the TDs they were going to bring over and hand out. Max was also ready to give us the guidelines on what to anticipate in the game.

When we entered the intergenerational learning center, I expected to find people quietly focused in front of computers, or maybe even reading old-fashioned books and being tutored by white haired elders.

Then I remembered what Joelle said about learning being different here.

I sensed a different level of engagement between instructor and learner than what I was familiar with. There seemed to be genuine passion on both sides for the topic being discussed. When someone appeared to be struggling with a subject, the person I perceived as the teacher was using creative approaches to bring it to life for the student. In some cases it was hard to tell which ones were the students and which were the teachers. Truly the transfer of information went in both directions. Sometimes people were playing games as a way to learn new concepts, strategies, and useful life skills. In other sectors of the center, I could see live discussions taking place via video with different cultural groups somewhere else on the planet. Now, this kind of education makes sense to me.

Max had us take seats in one of the classrooms and I could see the box of TDs had already been delivered and were sitting on a table in the front of the room. He picked up the box and passed them out to us.

Max launched right into his orientation, "First I will give you the information on what functions your TD performs. Remember that TD stands for Transaction Device, which you will want to have on you at all times. You will understand more about that in a moment. For ease in keeping them on you, I will give each of you a belt pouch, which any belt should slip through. I am also giving you a pouch with a strap, which you can wear around your neck or over your shoulder. Of course, there will be times when you will want to take them off, such as when you're sleeping. There are TD bays next to each of your sleeping accommodations. So long as it is within six feet of your body, it will be registering your field."

I wondered why it needed to be registering my field and I guess others in the orientation had the same question because Max said, "I'll get to that question in just a minute."

Max rolled out a thin piece of what I would later find out was glass and adhered it to the wall. It came on just like a computer screen with a 3D image of the TD, which would light up in the area he was referring to, as he went over the functions.

"The basic functions are as follows," he said, as he pointed to the bulleted list on the screen next to the image.

Basic features on the TD:

- Operates your transport vehicle.

  "Each vehicle is linked to a specific TD and can only be operated by the authorized user or users. Groups of three of you will share one vehicle. The model of vehicle you will be sharing are 4-seaters, to make it easier to go places together. Remember they can be operated automatically by telling the GPS on your TD where you want to go and it will take you there. We do not suggest that you operate them on manual until you understand how to responsibly use your thoughts, since **everything** here is thought responsive. I will tell you who you are sharing a vehicle with at the end of the orientation.

  When you press the transport vehicle icon on your TD, you simply say 'activate' and the vehicle should come to where you are. If it doesn't, check your TD screen to see if there is a message that says, 'in use.' It will show you who is using the vehicle and you can contact them to coordinate a trade off or pick up."

- Access to the teleportation system.

  "The teleportation system is just what you might imagine. The main teleportation pad is in the community center next to the business center. Packages for items people order online are teleported to the main pad at the business center. If you want to teleport yourself somewhere, you just have to find an available location and, before stepping onto the transport deck, enter the coordinates of where you want to go. You can use the GPS function on your TD to find a teleportation center. It will also tell you what the expected wait might be."

- As a GPS.

"This is probably still pretty similar to what you are familiar with. Basically, you just talk to it and tell it where you want to go, or what you want to find. There is a bay in the transport vehicle that your TD drops into for automatic navigation to the coordinates you have given."

- As a telecommunication device.

"Again, this will be about the same as the smart phones you are used to using. If you have problems, come by the welcome center and we will be happy to help you."

- As an energy meter for registering your credits and debits in your transaction account.

"Okay, so this is the part that is going to be the most foreign to you. I will give you the basics of the transaction account, but you may want to come back to the intergenerational learning center to learn more about how our monetary system works.

Basically, everyone is given a standard credit when they are born here. In your case, you have each been given that credit as what you might call a scholarship. Those scholarships are available to interdimensionals who are on the planet in your time-space reality to help bring humanity into resonance with the Earth at a higher frequency. In order to hold true to the possibilities for your future, it is valuable to have a deeply-rooted experience of what that looks and feels like, and that's why you are here. We wish to support you in that noble purpose.

The standard credit becomes sort of a slush fund for times when you may not be generating enough credits, an example of that might be if someone is in a rebalancing process, or what you might call sick. The easiest way for me to explain credits and debits is to use the analogy of a grid-tied, free energy power system. Let's use the example of a solar panel array. That system is metered and when you are generating energy from the sun, in excess of what you need, that goes into the grid. So, you now have an asset in your account. Then when the sun isn't shining, and you need power, you can draw on your account. Are you with me so far?" Max asked.

All heads indicated, yes.

"Well, we are all energy systems contributing to and receiving from 'the grid.' People here perform tasks to keep all of the aspects of the center operational based on what brings them joy. Joy is a unit of energy that can be measured and is valued as a contribution to the grid. By the way, credits are not given just for tasks. They are also obtained by positive thoughts, prayers for each other, and genuine acts of kindness that aren't done for the purpose of earning credits in the system.

If you want to purchase something in the community, that's an obvious debit to your transaction account. What might surprise you is that debits are also registered for negative energy, like thinking badly about someone, or not taking the time to help someone when it is easily within your power to do so. You can't trick the meter, because it is only measuring frequency, or bits of energy.

Now, let me give an example of what a transaction would look like in this community. Let's say someone loves weaving clothing, but doesn't necessarily want to use them. That person can make items available for purchase in the textile center. At the time they **produce** the item they are **credited** for it based on the amount of love they put into it while creating it."

Cali's hand shot up and Max paused to hear her question, "You mean you don't pay that person at the time someone actually purchases it, and you don't base the price on what the market has determined its value to be?"

"Good question, Cali," Max said, "hang with me and I hope I can make sense of it for you. To address your question specifically, we initially tried having a set price and then paying the artist when someone purchased it. However, we found that it stifled creativity if no one ended up wanting the item. Also, the artist's focus went to determining what they thought people would want. In other words it became more about making other people happy than doing what you love."

Max could see the confused looks on people's faces and he offered, "So you may be wondering how the price is determined on the items you purchase, if the artisan has already been paid. It is based on how much **you love** what you are purchasing. That amount then goes into the general account that the advance to the artisan was made from, to replenish it."

"What?" Sage said in a way that indicated having received a totally illogical answer, given her academic training and a predisposition to a capitalistic system. "So you're saying that if I really love something,

I am going to end up paying a lot more for it than it might be worth on the market? You could go through your transaction funds pretty quickly that way."

"It would seem so until you understand the broader picture," Max continued unruffled by the fidgeting in the room as people wrestled with something completely outside their knowledge base. "In actuality, it generates a higher quality of goods and it makes people more discerning about what they really want and need. Also, remember that each person has **equal** capacity to generate credits by doing what they love within the community.

On the other hand, if you are doing what you don't really want to do, but you think it will get you points, it is actually a slow drain on your transaction account. Once again, you can't fool the meter, so just be genuine and it will all balance out. You never have to worry that you won't have enough.

One last note, this system eliminates disproportionate wealth because taking advantage of other people for your own gain is a big debit in your transaction account. However, if a person is creating a lot of opportunities for others to apply their gifts, and to thrive offering them, they will receive abundant credits. It basically all takes care of itself and we find that the more joy is fed into the grid, the more our community thrives."

- Other entertainment or education apps of your choosing.

  "To wrap up, there are other entertainment and education apps you can add to your TD. You will find them at the telecommunication center for download.

Remember, the TDs are calibrated to your energy system and voice pattern, so they can only be used by you. If you lose or break one, you simply go to the telecommunication center, which is in the business center, and get a new one. They will calibrate the replacement to you and download your data, which is backed up in the cloud."

"Okay, let's take a fifteen minute break and then come back to go over the guidelines for the game."

We all got up for a stretch and bathroom breaks, which regardless of dimension still seems to be a necessity. I felt like someone had just given me a pass to the universal playground and everyone else seemed to feel the same by the way they were adoringly cradling their new TDs. I was wondering if it might not have been smarter to give us the TDs after the orientation to the game, but then these people seem to have things pretty well figured out.

Max sent a group message to our TDs, since he could count on getting our attention that way. "Please return to your seats for the remainder of the orientation."

We all filed back in and sat down, curious to find out what this game is all about. This portion didn't have any visual presentation with it, or handouts.

"You have probably all been wondering what this game is that you have been hearing about. The primary thing to know is that it is meant to be fun and to help you answer the question you came with. The best way to approach it is to explore this community based on what interests you, rather than being overly focused on the game and where clues will be coming from. An analogy that may make sense for some of you is that it is like the *Magic Eye* books where there is a 3D image camouflaged within an abstract graphic image. You can't see the 3D image emerge until you soften and change your way of looking.

The clues you will receive may be obvious, or they may be obscure, so don't discount anything as unimportant. The key to being ready for the next clue is being present and paying attention. That means, if you are on your way to a specific point and you notice something peripherally that catches your attention, then take a moment to explore that. Exploring that might mean going over and talking to someone you don't know.

For example, you may have been approached by a member of the community who hands you a feather and says something like, 'birds of a feather stick together.' Then you happen to see someone in one of the nooks in the community center who has the same kind of feather stuck down the spine of the book they are reading. Maybe the title of the book they are reading has a message for you, or maybe you need to strike up a conversation about the feather.

Remember, that everyone in the community is part of the game. Often, community members will have a thought occur that seems random, but we have learned to trust how we are used to deliver messages for each other's benefit, even though we may not understand it at the time. It's just a feeling you learn to follow. So, a clue may not be pre-planned. Receiving this type of information tends to happen more as you advance in the level of the game. As a part of your voice scan, we have determined which level of the game you are ready for, with the intention that all players have a good time and succeed.

There is no time limit, and you can ask each other or anyone in the community for help. You aren't **competing** against anyone, so just relax and take your time. You will all finish at different times, but finishing early doesn't get you extra points.

So, the summary of how to play the game is:

- Be fully present at all times.
- Learn to utilize all of your senses and pay attention to every nuance that stands out.

- Allow for the possibility that **everything** is connected to your greater understanding, even if it doesn't initially grab you as related to your question.
- Anticipate that people you don't know will be kind and helpful.
- Have fun deciphering the clues.
- Work together with others playing the game to resolve cryptic information more quickly, because your questions overlap.
- Be appreciative that you are still in the game, even when it seems to be taking you a long time to figure something out.
- Trust your feelings over logic.
- Anticipate magic when you begin each day.
- Relax and enjoy getting familiar with this place without trying to see how everything ties into the game. Sometimes when you least expect it, you will stumble on something significant.
- Only if you ignore all of the above will you get frustrated and quit.

Are there any questions at this point?" Max asked.

Everyone was silent. I know I was curious about what was going to come next, feeling like I had already learned so much from being in this place.

"Good enough," he said. "We are glad to have you and we hope your time here will be life-changing."

CHAPTER 8

The Hidden Temple

As the orientation concluded, and we gathered our few things, I could feel the sense of general overwhelm among the group in terms of not really knowing where to start exploring this fascinating new reality. Sage and Kai seem to have been here a bit longer than the rest of us, and they offered to help bring the newest members of our group up to speed with getting familiar with the place. We split off into two groups so we wouldn't be an obvious group of fledgling explorers bumbling around en masse. I also got that none of us felt ready to start interjecting ourselves into the social fabric here alone.

Our groups fell together naturally, maybe sensing an overlapping purpose, as Max had mentioned. Cali, Luna and Sage formed a group. Kai, Zander and I were a second team of sorts. Before we left the orientation room, Max reminded us to check the list at the front of the room for who we would be sharing transport vehicles with. I was thinking maybe we would have to reshuffle our groups, but we had intuitively grouped in the same way the vehicle assignments were made.

I'm becoming aware of how easily everything flows here just by following what feels right. I think it's that shift in focus from head to heart Joelle and I had touched on this morning.

I also feel unprepared for how to best support Zander, because I have limited experience with autism spectrum challenges. I'm wondering why in this "upgraded" dimension some people are still dealing with physical issues. This whole interdimensional thing is a mystery to me.

Kai got that the first thing the two of us needed to do was to check in with Zander, since it was obvious the compressed entry experience was a lot for him to process. I'm glad to have Kai paired up with us because he is a little older, probably twenty, and has that Aloha vibe that I associate with Hawai'ians, which just brings a sense of calm. The perplexing question for me really is, "How did Zander end up here and why?"

"Zander," I said, as I sat next to him, with Kai standing off to my side, "What do you most need right now?"

He was looking ahead at the floor and it was obvious he didn't want to make eye contact with either one of us. He was fidgety and I noticed he was clutching a folded piece of paper in his hand.

"Zander, is that something you would be willing to let us see?" I asked, as I glanced up at Kai with a look to convey, maybe this will tell us something.

Zander relaxed his hand and let me take the piece of paper. I knew that he could use language because he had spoken enough to have a voice scan when Trevor was with him. Maybe it was Trevor's centered presence and way of putting people at ease that had made that possible, but right now Zander didn't want to say much. I unfolded the paper slowly and reverently, getting that this was something of great importance to him. I never expected to see what was there... an intricate pen and ink drawing of Escalante de Luz with all of the pods, including details like the columned pathway with opened books to the intergenerational learning center. The only thing that looked out of place was what appeared to be some type of temple. The front wall of the primary triangular structure had one solitary pane of glass etched as a magnificent tree. A second windowless triangle behind it completed the building. In the picture, the structure was sitting in the middle of an old cottonwood grove.

I looked over at Kai and said, "This looks like Escalante de Luz, except for this," as I pointed to the pyramid shaped building.

Kai responded, "That's the Temple to the Divine. It sits out in the cottonwood grove just past the rejuvenation rooms."

Our mouths were both gaping open and now we were all speechless.

"Zander did you draw this picture?" Kai asked.

Zander nodded, yes.

"And you brought it through with you when you came here?" Kai inquired respectfully.

Again, he nodded, yes.

"Do you want to go to the shared space where people here make art?" I queried.

Zander looked up and quietly said, "Not yet, first I want to go here," as he pointed to the temple in the trees.

I realized that I have a lot to learn, beginning with reframing what I had considered to be special needs or challenges prior to coming here. What if instead we thought of them as children with special gifts and then stretched ourselves to understand **their** world?

"I haven't been to that temple yet, so that sounds perfect," I said, appreciating the company I was in.

Kai nodded his approval as well, saying "It's about a fifteen minute walk. Does that work for both of you?"

"Absolutely," I said. "Walking helps me connect with a place."

Kai smiled and said, "malama ka 'aina."

"What does that mean?" Zander asked, letting his body relax into the bubble of calm he felt himself bathed in by Kai and me.

"It is a basic understanding of my people that means love, and live in harmony with, the land. Walking puts us at a pace where her words can be heard through the elements, such as the whispers in the wind."

Zander said, "I'm good with walking to the temple… let's go."

We silently walked the community center paths to where they ended and then followed the winding dirt trail into the trees. I had gotten a bit ahead of Kai and Zander. About a hundred yards from the temple, a tapa cloth, with what appeared to be sacred markings was laid on the ground with simple fresh offerings of fruits, nuts and little sandwiches on sprouted bread. Around the food was a string of some kind of large brown polished wooden beads. I could see there was a note with it and I picked it up and read it, as I waited for the other two to catch up.

As they approached, Kai was particularly interested in what was there, recognizing how out of place it was. He saw me reading the note and asked, "What does it say?"

"It says, 'Offerings to nurture your bodies, as you prepare to nurture your souls,'" I said, intrigued by how someone could have known we were coming here and prepared this when we only decided to come fifteen minutes ago.

"I think this is for you, isn't it Kai?" I said, recognizing that it would have particular significance for him.

"Yes and no," he said, as he reached down and picked up the strand of glossy brown beads. "This is a Kukui ano ano or Kukui seed lei. The spiritual meaning of it is light, hope and renewal. In addition to it being a beautiful lei, it is used as prayer beads and it becomes more beautiful over time with the prayers held in it. It is also for protection."

Kai turned to Zander and said, "I believe this is for you. May I?" he asked as he held the lei up indicating he would like to place it around Zander's neck.

Zander rather awkwardly said, "Uh, ya, okay I guess," barely yielding the rigidity in his tall, lanky frame as he reluctantly let Kai drape it over his head.

"When we go into the temple, I will take the tapa cloth to place on the altar with any remaining food we haven't eaten," Kai said, as he motioned to the ground, inviting us to eat.

Kai walked to the side of where we were sitting. His arms were relaxed at his sides but with the palms open to the front of him. He began to chant, closing his eyes as he dropped into a place of total stillness from which pure beingness flows. The words were unfamiliar, but the powerful reverence they conveyed was unmistakable, and a chill ran up my spine. It was like the blessing before a meal, but more, and Zander and I knew not to help ourselves to the food until he was complete.

Kai opened his eyes after finishing the chant and just stood there for a few moments, as if he was listening and waiting for a reply. Just then a small blue songbird flitted from the tree we were seated next to and swooped down to pick up a seed from the tapa cloth.

When it felt appropriate, I quietly said, "That was beautiful. Can you tell us about it?"

At this point, Zander was noticing his hunger and picked up one of the sandwiches and began eating. His eyes were fixed on the temple but darted occasionally in Kai's direction, obviously curious about what he had to say.

"The chant is one of many I learned from my kumu. A kumu is a teacher and what they teach is indicated by what follows kumu, for example kumu hula is the teacher of the traditional dance. Kumu oli is a teacher of the chants, which are the sacred stories of our people. Since the hula doesn't have meaning without the chants or stories, it is most common to just say my kumu or kumu hula. Anyway, I was one of the youth in a group for youth leadership my kumu had started to help us remember the traditional stories of our people, and to use them as a foundation for creating the new story. He taught us the protocol of chanting to ask permission to enter a space, whether it is a building or a natural setting. The chant is done whether or not any people are physically present in the space. We ask permission to enter from **all** energies that are there. Then you wait for a sign or a feeling sense that you have been received. It is a protocol of respect and being conscious of where you are at all times.

I obviously don't stop and chant each time I go to a friend's house, to the grocery store, or to other routine locations. I tend to do it when I sense I am in the presence of something new... something powerful... something sacred. It is also a way of bringing me into the now with greater awareness, so that I don't harm myself or others by being fragmented. In this particular place, it is to acknowledge the energies of those who dwell here in spirit, or who have visited here with their offerings of love and gratitude.

"So, what is the question you are here to answer?... If you don't mind my asking," I said, mystified by why he would have come here when he seems so well guided by his kumu in the other dimension.

"I guess there is a two-part answer to that question. First of all, I think that most of us, the interdimensionals, who have synced up with this dimension are more found, than we are lost. But, the time-space reality we were born into is still working through some pretty dense stuff. It can feel impossible at times to pull away from the magnetic of the heavier emotions of fear, separation, and not enoughness in the collective field, and we start to identify with them.

Even those who try to cut themselves off from being bombarded by the negative messages of the world, still feel the weight of the limiting story. Trying to manifest anything different can feel like swimming through quicksand. Max said it in the orientation. We are here to get familiar with what it feels like to live in the **future** possibility, so when we return to our previous time-space reality, we have more conviction to fulfill our individual purposes. It's like when my sister used to tape her radio dial to the channel she wanted, because the slightest nudge would change the frequency and it would get staticky. So, we are basically here to tape ourselves to this frequency.

As far as my question for the game, it has to do with how the stories of my people can translate in a larger context and influence the choices that are being made." Kai paused and sort of sighed, "That was probably a lot more than you wanted to hear, and I know Zander was anxious to get here, so let's finish eating and go in."

I was ready to go on, but I couldn't help thinking about what Kai had just shared and how it related to the difference I was experiencing here when doubts would arise in me about not being able to live up to people's expectations of me. It's like there was no place for the thought to land... no power supply to energize it... Hmm, curious.

There was an apple and a few almonds left over after we had eaten all that we wanted. Kai gathered them up with the tapa cloth to place on the front altar inside. As we entered the back windowless section of the temple, it felt very cool and cave like. Motion detectors sensed our entry and small light fixtures, like those over artwork, softly illuminated the various alcoves. Each one paid homage to the avatars and saints of the different religious traditions throughout time. None of the religious icons took priority on the open, front altar. Instead there was a sense that all holy beings had come in service to the Earth, as depicted by the Tree of Life spreading its arms across the one massive altar window. I imagined that at the right time of day, the sun's angled rays would illuminate the heart of the temple, as they streamed through the etched branches of the tree.

Kai went directly to the altar to leave the tapa and the offerings we were passing on from what had been gifted us. He noticed there was a thin book laid open on a long wooden table at the base of the stairs leading up to the altar, and he went over to look at it. I had been making a more general sweep around the outer walls, appreciating the overall feeling of peace. Zander was seated near the alcove with Christ and appeared to be praying. Whatever was in the book on the table, it seemed to have caught Kai's attention and he set down what he was holding to pick it up and read it.

I could see the title of the book as I approached, *I Dreamed I Was Normal,* and I commented, "That seems like an unusual title for a book in a temple."

Kai flipped the book around to see the title and said, "Ya, it is, and I believe it was left as a clue for us to help Zander play the game."

"Why, what does it say?"

"It's about a woman who works with autistic children and how she discovers that she can communicate with this one boy by having him guide her hand on a computer keyboard to type out what he wants to say. He tells her that autistic children connect with each other in dreamtime, because there they are free of the challenges they have in their bodies, thus *I Dreamed I Was Normal.* He also tells her that he can come into her dreams, if she focuses on meeting him there. She ends up being able to do it after trying a few times and, following a very real experience with him in her dreams, she tells him about it and he guides her hand to type out, 'you did it,'" Kai summarized.

"So, do you think this is telling us to take Zander to the business or learning center so we can use a keyboard to have him help us understand what he needs?" I pondered, as I got used to playing detective.

"No, I don't think so," Kai said and I could almost see the wheels in his mind turning. "He speaks if he wants to, and he obviously communicates through drawing. I think this whole **game** idea is overwhelming to him. I mean, nothing is familiar to any of us, and for him it seems particularly challenging. I think this clue is suggesting that we help navigate him to an environment that will feel safe for him to interact with the people in the community."

Then I put it together, "The collective dream space!"

"I guess I missed that on my tour of the community," Kai said, "Where is it?"

"It's in the observatory."

"Do they do it every night?" Kai asked.

"I don't know. Maybe we can use the GPS function on the TD to see if we can get schedule information," I suggested, as I pulled out my TD, pressed the GPS icon and asked for the schedule for collective

91

dreaming in the observatory. Immediately it came up and it seemed they only did it once a week.

"Do you know what day it is?" I asked Kai, realizing I had no reference point for that since my arrival.

Kai had a similarly confused look on his face as well, but just then my TD beeped and I looked down to see that it was highlighting the day we were on.

"We're in luck," I said, "There's one tonight."

"Do we need to reserve a space?" Kai wondered out loud.

I lifted the TD back up to voice level, about ready to ask it to call the observatory, when a message flashed across the screen. "Reservation for three confirmed for 9 pm."

Kai and I glanced at each other, shook our heads with a look of amazement and simultaneously said, "Wow!... These people are way ahead of us."

We turned to see if we could spot Zander in the dimly lit back section of the temple. He was done praying and he was tiptoeing around the space checking out the other alcoves. I would have thought the tiptoeing was a gesture of reverence in the temple, but I had noticed him tiptoeing in the other buildings we had been in during orientation. It was almost like he was trying not to be heard in hopes that he would also not be seen. I also realized that he was still wearing what I presumed to be the standard issue for males arriving through the portal. It was the same material as the shift I had been given when I arrived. I did notice that he had on some basic slip-on shoes, sort of like Chinese martial art shoes. My guess is that given the community's awareness of Zander's sensitivities to touch, they had provided what would be most comfortable.

"Zander," I said, "I know a lot has happened for you today, but I want to check in with you to make sure you are comfortable in what you are wearing. We can go and find some other clothes for you, if you want to have more choices of things to wear."

"No, no," he said, shaking his head. "This feels good."

"What about a hoodie or something soft to cover your arms for when it gets cooler tonight?" I said, surprised by how motherly I had become after being given the responsibility of helping Zander.

"Um, I don't know," he said.

"Well, would you feel comfortable going to the re-use store and hanging out while I look for some things for myself? And, Kai, are you wanting to hang with us until we go to the observatory tonight?" I asked, as I turned to check in with him.

"I could, but I would prefer to go over to the Rawsome Café to play chess with someone I met there yesterday, who said she would be there again today," he confessed.

"I'm cool with that," I replied, actually relieved that I could spend more time at the re-use center without worrying about Kai being bored.

"Zander, another option is that I could take you to the art studios and find a place for you to draw while I do my shopping."

I could see him struggling with the choice, and I was picking up his stress of being alone in another place he was unfamiliar with, even though drawing was a better way for him to express what was going on. It's not like he knew me or Kai well either, but we had managed to establish a basis of trust.

"I'll go with you," Zander said hesitantly.

"Okay, sweet," I said, thinking maybe he would change his mind about a hoodie or something like that, if we found the right thing.

"Kai, maybe we'll see you at the Rawsome Café later. We won't interrupt your chess game though," I said, in sort of a little sister teasing way, hoping to see if I could get a reaction that would indicate what kind of interest he had in this new "friend."

The next hour and a half flew by as I picked my way through the treasures at the re-use center. Zander pretty much sat on a chair in the corner by the dressing rooms playing around with his new TD. I was able, however, to get him to try on a couple of hoodies and found one that met with his approval. I am also really diggin this whole transaction account system and how easy it is to make a purchase, and I am surprised to see I have already registered a credit today.

Just as we were leaving the re-use store, I thought it would be good to take my purchases back to my room. Then I realized that Trevor had rushed back from the canyon with Zander to get him to the orientation this morning and probably hadn't had time to show him to his guestroom. It seemed that no sooner had I thought that when we ran into Trevor.

"I thought I might find you here," he said. "Did you find some more treasures?"

"Ya," I said, almost guilty for the abundance I was now experiencing.

"Oooh, be mindful," he said lightly, "That guilt will create a debit in your transaction account, and you don't want to wipe out the credit you've already gotten."

"Ya, what's that about anyway?" I asked, glad that he brought it up.

"It's for your willingness to help Zander get oriented here," he explained.

"I can see that this transaction account could pretty quickly make a person aware of where their thoughts are. So, basically, every time I judge myself or someone else, feel jealous, inadequate, or whatever, it's going to show up as a debit, right?" I probed further.

"Yep, and all of the better feeling thoughts are going to show up as credits. It's a great way to build awareness because it is completely objective. You can't get upset with a meter for registering energy, but you might get bent out of shape by someone pointing out what you're not seeing," Trevor explained.

Trevor then turned his attention to Zander. "Today has probably been a bit of a rough day with so much change so fast, ya?"

"It's okay," Zander said, "It doesn't feel so loud and prickly here."

"It will get even better," Trevor said kindly. "The frequency of this place should feel more familiar and safe to you than where you came from, but it could take a little while to fully repair the sensory overload and conditioned reactive patterns."

"That's actually true for all of you, to some extent," Trevor said, speaking more to me. "The difference with Zander is that his sensory sensitivities were activated at a higher level before coming here and so it was harder for him to filter out the harsh overstimulation of your dimension.

Anyway, Zander, I was wondering if you would like me to take you to the room you will be staying in while you're here?"

"Ya, that would be good," he said, looking like he was ready for some downtime.

"Zander, Kai and I have a reservation tonight for the collective dreaming in the observatory," I said, wondering how to find Zander later to get him over to that pod.

"The contact information for everyone from the orientation this morning has been programmed into each of your TDs so you can easily find each other. While you're in the GPS function, you just say find Zander and it will show you where he is."

Trevor said to Zander, "Right this way," and they headed off in the direction of the guestrooms.

He turned back around to me, as I stood there wondering what I was going to do next and said, "Have a great time tonight! In the meantime, I highly recommend the rejuvenation rooms, if you haven't tried them."

CHAPTER 9

Into the Dream

After dropping off my new wardrobe items in my room, I decided to take Trevor's recommendation to check out the rejuvenation rooms before the collective dreaming tonight. I knew that they were near the path we took earlier today out to the temple, so I made my way into the northeast part of the center so I could get back there. I didn't know if I needed to book ahead, but I figured I would just take my chances and, if it was in the flow, one would be available.

I also wanted to take my time getting there. I thought I'd locate one of the little reading nooks sculpted into the interior cob walls in the main building, so I could be a fly on the wall and get more of the overall vibe of the place. As I meandered through, I found just the right one with natural light from a small skylight above. It had a comfortable southwestern chair, like the one in my guestroom. I also had a good view of the central atrium from here.

More often than not, people were walking two and three together, although I noticed that they were often intersecting for only a part of the way to each of their destinations. No one seemed to be in a hurry. What struck me most was the amount of genuine laughter... the kind from the belly that makes you want to join in, rather than the kind that rings hollow of joy but stills hopes to make a connection.

What also impressed me were the number of kids, probably from about age ten and up, who were coming and going alone from the various pods. My initial thought was that it probably had to do with the parents being able to locate their kids at any time using their TD, the way Trevor had shown me to find the other interdimensionals; but when I felt more deeply into what was happening it was just an overall sense of safety. But, no, that wasn't even it, because to feel safe there would need to be a threat that one is safe from. The sense of potential threat was just absent. I also got that people knew each other in a deeply connected way, even if their daily interactions were brief. The presence they had to really **hear** each other in that handful of minutes could fill more empty space than a lifetime with someone who never saw you.

I also loved that I didn't stand out as a person of color in a predominantly white culture. This is a truly blended world. No one ever looked at me with suspicion when I would come into a shop alone. Yet, I could still feel the residue of deep wounds carried through generations. It's going to take me some time to learn how to use my words to speak power to the people, when there is no lack of that here.

I let my attention turn to the butterflies in the atrium and didn't notice the colorful kickball that had caught the edge of my nook and twirled in, until it bounced off my foot. A little curly locked blond girl with big brown eyes came to retrieve her ball and saw me sitting there.

"Sorry," she said, noticing me admiring the butterflies.

"What's your name?" she quizzically asked.

"Chrysalis. What's yours?"

"Trina... Did your parents love butterflies?" she asked with the innocent curiosity of a young child.

"I suppose they did. Are you asking because of my name?"

"Uh-huh," she said, nodding her head as curls bounced playfully.

"They didn't give me that name. My name was Chris, but I liked Chrysalis better."

"You look like you tell good stories. Will you tell me one?" Trina asked, as if we both had all the time in the world.

"Okay. What's the subject?" I asked her.

"Butterflies, of course."

We spent the next ten minutes in the magical world of butterflies and Trina, feeling satisfied, picked up her ball and ran back in the direction she came from.

I felt complete in the space I was occupying and moved on to find the rejuvenation rooms. My mind also flashed on what both Trevor and Max said about everyone in the community being a part of the game, and it made me wonder if that included Trina. There was definitely information coming that was resonating with me, but it wasn't the kind of cut-and-dried, one-dimensional questions and answers I was used to. It was a story weaving together and it was hard to tell what was part of the game and what wasn't.

I arrived at the rejuvenation rooms just as a small built, thirty something guy was coming out of one. He saw me trying to figure out how to read the electronic schedule posted next to the door and how to make a reservation.

"Is this your first time here?" he asked, as a way to let me invite his help.

"Ya, I guess that's kinda obvious, huh?"

"A little," he said warmly. "Do you want me to show you how it works?"

"That'd be great!" I said with relief.

"Okay, just press the icon here that says, 'schedule' and it will display today's openings. The schedule is only for the day and it is on a first come, first served basis. Okay, so you can see that the room I just came out of is available for the next thirty minutes. Do you want to take that slot?"

"Ya, that would be awesome!"

"So, what you want to do is take your TD and press the transaction account icon, then you pass this top edge of the TD across the opening on the schedule and it notes the transaction and books your spot. It's that easy."

"Amazing!… Thank you so much for your help."

"No worries," he said, "Enjoy!"

I saw the transaction register as a debit in my account and also noticed I had another credit that was logged fifteen minutes ago. Had I gotten a credit for taking the time to tell Trina a story?

The rejuvenation room was so amazing. The one I entered had a mineral hot tub that was concrete lined. I wouldn't have been surprised if it was the same type of photocatalytic concrete I saw in the path to the observatory, because there appeared to be ultraviolet lights around the inside rim, shining down in. The tub was sunken into the floor, with indented spaces in the side for footholds and a curved handrail like you would find for getting in and out of a swimming pool. The varied size river rocks in the floor provided a reflexology treatment when I walked barefoot on them. There was a shower head coming out of the resin sealed, wood paneled wall, with a drain in the river rock floor below. There was no enclosure for the shower; it was just part of the open room. There were rice paper sliding panels on the opposite wall of the room that opened onto a beautiful garden of golden bamboo, and a lily pad adorned koi pond. There was a small, Japanese cast iron teapot on a hot plate with little tea cups next to it, and also a zazen cushion on a raised cherry wood platform next to the sliding doors for meditation.

As I sat soaking up the goodness of the hot tub, I noticed an interesting, well-worn dirt path that didn't seem to go anywhere. It appeared to be an infinity symbol beginning and ending just past the koi pond. I felt a resonance with it and stored it in my information banks, curious to see what more might come related to it.

I collected my few things and made my way back toward the guestrooms to round up Zander. I used my TD to locate him and saw that he was still in his guestroom. I sent him a voice message by speaking into my TD using the telecom feature. "I can pick you up soon to wander around a bit before we go to the collective dreaming at the observatory. Can you be ready in ten minutes and are you hungry?"

"I can be ready. I had some food at the drive-through window in my room," Zander's message came back.

I blurted out a laugh, thinking what a funny and appropriate way it was to describe the hidden, food automat in the wall of the guestrooms. It was hard for me to know at this point if Zander intended the humor. I certainly didn't want him to think I was making fun of him, so, I said, "That's a perfect description for those hidden windows. I'm going to remember that because it made me laugh."

We had arranged to meet Kai at the observatory. Zander and I took our time wandering through the center, as I gave him the tour of the features, based on my vast knowledge of almost two days here. It's a bit hard to believe it's only been that long, given how much this feels like home.

This time along the path to the observatory, I got to walk among the stars since the darkness of the sky had made the lights in the pathway visible. The roof of the observatory had been retracted for those who wanted to spend time viewing the heavens above. It was a perfect clear night for it with only a sliver of a new moon.

We checked in at the front reception area and entered the observatory. From the number of places that were arranged, it looked like there were going to be seven of us dreaming together tonight. Each place had a meditation cushion for sitting and a type of mummy-bag cocoon laid on top of a very cushy looking pad. It appeared we were going to sit in circle first and then go into dreaming. There was a Native American grandmother gathering a turtle rattle, a colorfully woven blanket and a sage stick into the center of the circle.

Kai had arrived and we placed ourselves on each side of Zander in the circle. I noticed that Sage, from the orientation, was also here. She looked to be part Native American, although there also appeared to be some Caucasian and Asian mix in there as well. From her question in the orientation about the money system, I get that this nonlinear ritual setting might be a good place to integrate her intellectual and spiritual sides in this new reality.

After everyone settled in, the grandmother began chanting and rattling as she walked around the circle and saged each one of us. It felt energetically similar to the chant that Kai had offered earlier.

Grandmother Flora introduced herself as a Hopi elder. She said "The spiritual center **within** is a sacred site and our prophecies say it will have a special purpose in the future for mankind to survive."

As she spoke, I remembered learning about the Anasazi people, who lived in this southwest area and were said to have disappeared suddenly and without a trace. The name Anasazi comes from a Navajo word meaning "the ancient ones" and here was this ancient one sitting before us in this other dimensional reality. It made me wonder if the missing Anasazi had done a parallel migration, so to speak.

"When we are ready to enter the sacred dream together tonight, we will each silently set our personal intention for guidance. But first, I will share an important prophecy, which will have great meaning for those of you here who will play significant roles in helping us realize it," Grandmother Flora began.

"The prophecy is shared by many of the indigenous people from both North and South America. It is the prophecy of the eagle and the condor.

More than 500 years ago, before the predestined arrival of other members of the human family, there flourished vast civilizations that carried trade and commerce from the very north of the Americas to the very south of the Americas and across the Rockies and the Andes. This was a time of union between the condor and the eagle. The eagle represents indigenous people from the north, with their message and their knowledge. The eagle is a symbol of great meaning all over the world. It is a very masculine energy that discovers, invents and makes things happen. The eagle, from some perspectives can also represent the mind. That's why technology is so advanced in the north.

The condor represents indigenous people from the south. It's a mellower, softer energy. There's a lot of heart and a lot of connection with the Earth in the condor cultures.

So these were the two primary symbols of many of the indigenous peoples of the Americas. All of the varying prophecies of the different tribes foretold that a great spiritual wintertime was coming. And, as foreseen, members of the human family from afar came to these sacred lands. This was the time when the union of the condor and eagle was shattered. We had prayed as we were told to pray. We tried to live our lives in harmony with Mother Earth. We asked ourselves, 'Why were we punished?'

There have been wounds of injustice, of oppression, of colonization, of greed, of superstition, all those things that injure the human heart. And, the wound of that trauma has been carried for many generations. But it was also prophesied and promised that after a period of 500 years, a great, great spiritual springtime would emerge with such power and such intensity that all that had been covered in the cold, bitter snow would be revealed and cleansed and purified and that we would emerge, galvanized, reunited as not only a reunion of the condor and the eagle, but a reunion of the entire human family. The beginning time for that emergence is **the now that you have come from**, my young friends," she said as she moved her deeply penetrating, but gentle gaze around the circle to affirm the interdimensionals in the group.

"Thank you all for coming to share in the dreaming tonight. May our medicine be powerful and our dreams be good. Aho," she concluded, and made her way to her sleeping cocoon in the circle of seven.

The observatory roof was still opened to the night sky and a blue butterfly flitted through and down around the circle. I don't know a lot about butterflies, but I do know they don't typically fly at night.

"The polacca has come to dream with us," said Grandmother Flora. "It is good medicine, since the butterfly symbolizes humankind's spiritual transformation. We sleep in cocoons to make ready and these have the same fibers of monoatomic gold and platinum that are in the clothing you were given when you arrived. It is for balancing and creating alignment and harmony."

I was energized by what Grandmother Flora had shared, and I wasn't feeling like I could go to sleep for a while. I also remembered what Kai had read from the book left at the temple about focusing on being with Zander in the dream. It felt important to make that happen, if possible, so we could help him with clues that might come. The lights had been turned off and the comfort of the cocoon made for perfect star gazing. There was something about the combination of elements that made me feel like I was Dorothy in *The Wizard of Oz* when she was overcome by drowsiness in the poppy field. That was the last thing I remember before I fell into a deep sleep.

In the morning when I woke up, I remembered only bits and pieces of what I had dreamed. During the night someone had laid a sketch pad and colored pencils next to Zander and he was awake, busily drawing. Kai appeared to still be dreaming by the way I could see his eyeballs moving rapidly back and forth, as if watching images on a screen that were passing quickly. The rest of us were awake or starting to stir.

"When everyone is awake and ready we will take some time to share what we each saw in the dream and see what messages it carries for each of us. While you are waking up there is some guayusa tea for you to enjoy, which also helps bring more clarity with the dream. It is traditionally shared in the morning circle of some of the indigenous tribes in the Amazon who dream collectively," Grandmother Flora said quietly, so as not to alarm our still foggy senses.

The mood was quiet and reflective, and the overall feeling was that people didn't want to engage in conversation while they were still trying to hold the bits of dreams they had managed to grab. Now Kai was awake also. I was personally glad to have Grandmother Flora there to help guide us in piecing it all together and seeing the deeper meaning.

"Now that we have all returned from the dreamtime, please come back to your places in the circle," Grandma Flora requested.

Those who were milling about and those who had gone to make bathroom stops settled back in. She picked up the turtle shell rattle she had used to take us into the dreaming and held it reverently. It seemed every one of her actions were slow and purposeful, more at the pace of a persistent river carving a new path. Efficiency for her had more to do with respectful inclusion than completing a task quickly, checking it off and moving on.

"The turtle brings stories from the watery world of our subconscious, our emotions, our dreams, to the surface; and so I ask that each person hold this as it comes to you around the circle and share what seems significant from your dream. You may only have a few words to offer, but as each person speaks, it may help you to remember more and to see deeper meaning."

Grandmother Flora didn't ask who wanted to begin. She simply passed the turtle shell rattle to Kai, perhaps sensing how much he was downloading just before he woke. "Kai, will you begin and then pass to your left," she requested.

"I remember seeing the night sky and also the night rainbow, as happens on rare occasions where I am from. There were many of us gathered together. I was walking the rainbow as a bridge, but I don't know to where. Zander was there also and he was picking sage. There were also bees coming and going from a hive in an infinity pattern," Kai paused for a moment, scanning his memory to see if there was more to say at this time, and when he felt satisfied with his offering, he passed the turtle to Zander on his left.

Zander was making a few final marks on his drawing and he set the pencil down and accepted the turtle. "This is the easiest way for me to say what I saw," Zander said, as he held up the picture he had drawn with amazing detail in such a short time.

Grandmother Flora asked, "Would you be willing to pass it around, Zander?"

He nodded yes and passed it to me, on his left. I took a moment to look at it and noticed a few things that stood out. Since we weren't invited to comment on anyone else's sharing at this point, I noted them mentally and then passed the drawing on. When it made its way back to Zander, he passed the turtle rattle to me.

"My dream was sketchy. There were some images, but also a lot of sensations, primarily of being off balance. I did see the bamboo and koi pond that I had been at yesterday evening. I also saw the geometric patterns and felt the sensations in my feet, like when I was barefoot in the canyon with Trevor. Zander was also in the dream and he was standing in the middle of a teeter-totter with a young woman on one end and an older woman on the other balancing him. It seemed like the older woman was Joelle from the community and the younger one was maybe Sage?" I said uncertainly, as I looked in her direction. "I think that's it for me," I concluded and passed to the older woman on my left. I assumed that she and the man on the left of Sage, who looked like a cross between Adam Lambert and a yoga teacher, were members of the community.

"In my dream, there was a star port on top of the third mesa into the canyon and I was teaching a young crow how to fly to the heavens and bring back knowledge from the star people to benefit the land and the people who were sick. We were programming crystals to carry healing frequencies," spoke the mysterious, silver haired woman with bluer eyes than I had ever seen.

She then turned to Sage, gazing directly into her eyes as she passed the turtle. Even from where I sat, I could feel the electricity that arced across the suspended turtle held between their hands. Sage accepted it and turned back to face the center of the circle.

"In my dream, I was a bee and I was making honey and propolis for the hive. I was flying out and back to the hive in an infinity pattern. Then I changed into myself and I was balancing at the edge of a precipice as a great fire was approaching. Zander was with me and we were frozen in fear, certain that this ominous force was going to consume us. Then I heard, 'Get to the other side.' When I glanced back to look, it seemed too far to be able to leap across. Realizing that we would die in the approaching fire if we didn't try, we released our focus on the threat and turned to the other side. I looked at Zander, grabbed his hand and yelled, 'Jump!' and we made it!" Sage shared and then passed the turtle to the man on her left.

"In my dream, I was at the café and there was a young woman who was entertaining the patrons by making up stories about their lives. They would tell her whether the offering was accurate or not. Whether or not she was right, people enjoyed hearing the stories. Then, a great big orange cat came in and sat right in front of her, as if it was his turn for a story. She looked at him said, 'Which life do you want to know about?' The cat starting whirling around laughing, changed into a tiger, and said, 'This one.' The dream kept morphing into something that felt very bizarre and disconnected, so I'll just end with that," he said and passed the rattle to Grandmother Flora, who would complete the circle.

"In my dream, I saw the children of the night rainbow, which Kai spoke of. They were the people of many colors who held the knowledge from before recorded time… who remembered who they were and why they came. They had made it across the bridge and a great garden that had been planted many years before was flourishing."

She paused after sharing her dream and asked, "Did you see connections between your dreams, and did hearing others give you more insight into your own?"

We all indicated, yes.

"Grandmother, may I ask for your assistance in understanding pieces I picked up from each of the dreams, which I believe are directions for me?" Sage asked humbly.

"Tell me first what you perceived and I will see if I have more to add," Grandmother said.

"I have some knowledge of plant medicine from my grandmother, who is Crow, and I am also a researcher exploring the use of technology to deliver healing frequencies. Computer chips are crystalline and are, of course, programmable. So, I will find the third mesa in the canyon as suggested by our friend to my right. In Kai's dream, Zander is picking sage, which could mean me, and in Chrysalis' dream Zander is being balanced between me and another woman. In my own dream, I was with Zander helping him to escape danger and I'm wondering if the picture Zander drew is part of the healing center here? If so, I am getting the sense that I am to accompany him to it, both to assist him and for my own learning. I also noticed a common thread in the dreams with the bees and the infinity pattern and I'm not clear what this means."

"Your sensing is accurate," Grandmother Flora acknowledged. "The picture Zander drew does appear to be of the balance wheel in the wellness center that is run by Joelle, and your support of him is appreciated. The water in your body is also a carrier of information through its crystalline structure. That is why our New Zealand kin, the Waitaha emphasize the importance of how you carry your water, so keep that in mind related to healing work. The connection to the bees, which several of you picked up on, has to do with the Earth messengers who walk an infinity pattern near the gardens with the koi pond. They walk barefoot on the Earth each morning and receive information about disturbances in the Earth needing our attention. Those of you who saw that in the dream are invited to join them. I believe that was Kai, Chrysalis and you, Sage."

She continued, "The Earth messengers walk each morning about an hour past sunrise. They meet in the café after that to review the information they have received and to share social time. Joelle is one of the Earth messengers, so she will be there and she can tell you more about the wellness center. Drew helps run the café, and I believe he is probably headed there now," she said nodding toward the man I hadn't recognized in the circle. "He can introduce you to the Earth messengers when they complete their check-in this morning. In the meantime, it is a wonderful place to hang out and enjoy some breakfast."

"Thank you all for coming. Let us close the circle with a blessing," she said as we stood and joined hands. "Great Spirit, your gifts are many and we thank you for those you have given in our dreams. May we walk the good red road in the way of beauty, always knowing that all things are connected. Aho."

Grandmother Flora then went and stood facing the unidentified woman who had been seated next to me. They joined hands and a sphere of light seemed to envelope them. It was our cue to not linger in the space any longer. Drew was the only member from the community in the group, other than Grandmother Flora, and as we left Kai asked him who the mysterious woman was and Drew said, "I don't know. I've never seen her before."

CHAPTER 10

Rebalancing

As we passed back through the center to the café, it was already busy with activity. Maybe because I am sixteen, and love being creative with clothes, I enjoyed noticing the different ways people expressed themselves here. It definitely wasn't about fitting in with some generic fashion trend that everyone accepted, although there were a fair number of people who opted for the simple clothes like I received in the canyon. There were some styles I hadn't seen before, but they weren't space-age looking in the way I would have expected, if they were keeping pace with the technologies. This place is somewhat like being at a costume party with every time period and culture represented, depending on what someone felt like on a particular day. This is definitely people watcher's paradise.

I hadn't been into the café before and when we walked in, it instantly felt homey. It's like a big living room with overstuffed couches and chairs in congenial clusters. There are regular tables and booths for those eating food, and several are occupied by people playing games. I imagine little jam sessions or open mics on the currently vacant stage. There is also a book-lined nook for those wanting a break from electronic devices.

"Hey guys, where do you want to sit?" Drew asked as we walked through the café. "I'll introduce you to the Earth messengers when they are done debriefing. In the meantime, find a place to sit and feel free to order what you want... on the house. I'll send Sabrina over to get your orders."

We checked in with each other and chose a booth near a group of people I assumed were the Earth messengers, because I saw Joelle and also Trevor. I was curious about what they were discussing. It didn't feel like eavesdropping since everything here is so transparent. We'll find out soon enough anyway.

A really cute woman, probably late twenties, approached our table. Her style reminded me of Betty Boop... cropped black hair with little pin curls accenting her open round face and big eyes. She was carrying a tray of little shot glasses containing drinks in a range of questionably palatable colors.

"Good morning, everyone. I'm Sabrina and I'm here to take your breakfast orders. The specials here are really the energy drinks and, since I'm guessing this type of thing might be new for you, I brought some samples. This first one is the *Green Goddess*. It's cucumber, celery, ginger, lime, assorted leafy greens, cilantro, fennel root, banana, hemp hearts and coconut oil."

Sabrina pointed to the sample glass and all of our faces must have turned the same color, because she said, "It's actually one of the favorites! The next one is *Beet Grateful*. It has beets, carrots, cucumber, ginger and lime. The last of today's drink specials is the *Avo-tar*, which is avocado, red and green bell pepper, cucumber, celery, tomato, chard and lemon.

Standard beverages include guayusa tea, which you might be familiar with as yerba mate. We also have other herbal teas, coffee and apple or orange juice. Food items include some sprouted grain breads and cereals; fruit bowls; and raw, whole milk yogurt and kefir. You can also have a blueberry-peach or a pineapple-colada smoothie, with or without protein. And, of course, everything is organic."

I noticed Sage glancing over to the Earth messengers table to see if she could detect their beverage of choice and there were a number of glasses that appeared to have been the *Green Goddess* by the residue on the glass.

"I'll try a sample of the *Green Goddess*," she said tentatively and Sabrina handed her one of them. Sage chugged it like a strong whiskey, but rather than the relief one has when getting past the burn of the whiskey, her look was one of delighted surprise. "Wow, that's amazingly good!"

"Okay, I'll try the *Avo-tar* sample," Kai said, indicating his willingness to be a part of this bold experiment.

I also chimed in, "The *Beet Grateful* sounds good to me."

Zander sat looking at the samples, still not convinced by the rave reviews they were getting. By his expression, I was imagining he was thinking about the options in the "drive-through window" in his room, but those were healthy also. Somehow the packaging and window just made them seem more familiar.

"So, are you ready to order?" Sabrina asked?

Zander actually kicked off the ordering, "I'll have some yogurt, cereal and orange juice."

"I'm going to go for the *Green Goddess*," Sage said as if she had just passed the qualifying round for the Olympics.

"I'll take the pineapple-colada smoothie with protein," Kai added.

"I guess I'll have the *Beet Grateful* and a cup of yerba mate," I said, wrapping up the order.

"Great, I'll be right back with that," Sabrina said.

It occurred to me that with all of the advances in technology here and how automated so many things are, like the transport vehicles, teleporters, schedules and registration information, why do they still have people waiting tables? Seems like you could just come in, swipe your TD to put yourself on the list for a table, have it light up a table on a diagram to indicate where you were to sit, and then have a computerized menu pop up from the table, so you could just select the items you want. The bill could also appear on the electronic screen at the table and you just swipe it with your TD to debit your transaction account and walk out.

I shared what I was thinking with the others at the table and none of them really had any comment. There was an older gentleman sitting alone at the booth behind us. He and I were sitting back-to-back and he overheard the conversation. He had on a derby bowler hat with a red paisley hat band that matched his bowtie. He looked like he was dressed for something special with his crisp white shirt, a charcoal pin-striped jacket of fine wool and a gold watch fob chain dangling from the matching vest pocket. He wore thin, round wire rim glasses and as he turned to face us, a rosy beam of kindness was evident on his cheeks.

"Excuse me for interrupting, but I couldn't help hearing your conversation and I may be able to answer that question," he said as a way of asking for an invitation to continue.

"Great," all of us but Zander said.

"It's about the relationships… People don't necessarily come here for the food, although it's fantastic. They come here to be with each other and to have the opportunity to share a bit of kindness. Sabrina doesn't do this as a job to support herself, in the way you may be thinking. She does it because it is the most efficient way for her to touch many people in one day. People who live alone, like me, come here and are served a healthy dose of love. You can't do that with automation."

He paused for a moment and pulled something out of his pocket. "By the way, my name is Will and when the moon is beginning to get full, have **her** come see me. The butterfly in the observatory can show her the way," he concluded cryptically as he handed me the card.

Will then slipped out of his booth, tipped his hat to us and left the café. We all sat there perplexed by the last bit of what he had to say.

"That seems like a clue," I said and the others nodded in agreement, "but for which one of us?

He did make a point of stressing **her** when he was referring to the moon. If the card was for one of us he would have surely handed it to who it was for, but he said **her** indicating someone who is not here."

Sage got a look on her face like a light bulb had just gone on. "Luna, the moon is Luna. She is in my transport vehicle group and we spent the afternoon together after the orientation."

"Did you guys happen to talk about your questions for the game?" Kai asked curiously.

"Ya, actually we did," Sage said, as she seemed to be mentally reviewing what they had talked about.

"Would you mind sharing what Luna's question was?" Kai asked.

Sage thought about it for a minute, wondering if she would be breaking confidence. "I guess that feels okay, especially since Max said that our purposes overlap and that part of succeeding in the game is to trust each other and to work as a team to decipher clues. This community is so different. I don't get that anyone here would use information with the intent to harm anyone else. I'm also still adjusting to how transparent everything is and so the idea of keeping a thought private is kind of a joke."

"Not to mention that people would lose credits in their transaction accounts if they used information in a harmful way," I pointed out.

"So, anyway, Luna is a community revitalization activist who came from a place where the local economy had collapsed. There was no assistance from government or industry and the people had to find ways to reinvent themselves. In addition, community is central to her Latina roots and part of her question is how she can help to keep person-to-person relationship and real community alive in a world that has become very virtual," Sage shared.

"Bingo!" Kai exclaimed, "Seems like a fit with the information Will just gave. Sage, can you pass the card and clue on to Luna, since you guys are hanging together?… Is that okay with you Chrysalis?"

"Ya, sure. Maybe Will handed it to me because I was sitting closest to him."

Sabrina was bringing our food over with Drew right behind her. The Earth messenger group was breaking up, and he wanted to introduce us before they headed off in different directions. Sabrina set our orders down on the table and Drew continued on to a large roundtable area kitty-corner from our booth.

"Hey everyone, before you leave, I would like to introduce you to some of our visitors who were guided in the collective dreaming last night to join you in walking the infinity path," Drew explained to the Earth messengers.

"They just got their food and they are at the table right there. I know that some of you have already met. Anyway, would it work to go over there with me so I can make a quick round of introductions? Then you can tell them what they will need to know to join you tomorrow."

I could see they were all nodding and collecting their things to follow Drew.

Drew began by going around our table and introducing us. "This is Sage, Kai, Chrysalis and Zander. Zander won't be one of the walkers, but they all just came together from the collective dreaming and I believe he would like to connect with you, Joelle, before you leave."

Since Drew had just brought Joelle into the introductions via the reference to Zander, he officially introduced her to the whole group.

He then moved on, placing his hand on Trevor's shoulder, "I know you have all met Trevor, Earth messenger and entry host extraordinaire."

Next, he introduced a striking, older woman in a colorful, southwestern style skirt and sleeveless blouse with a mane of silver white hair swept up in a turquoise inlaid clip, against radiant, sienna toned skin and sea green eyes. "This is Michele. She is the senior Earth messenger and our coordinator for communications within the community and between the global pods of messengers. You will learn more about that tomorrow."

"This is Luis..." Drew said.

My mind had already jumped ahead with a narrative about Luis... handsome, early-thirties Latino guy whose lean muscular build, cropped hair and calloused hands make me think me might be a rock climber.

"… He's our master gardener in the organic gardens outside the café. If there is anything you want to know about healing yourself and the Earth while growing food, he's the one to ask."

Nearing the end of the group, Drew put his hand out and motioned toward a man I'm guessing to be forty but, with as healthy as everyone is, it's really hard to tell age. He has honey blond hair and brown eyes that feel like pools of wisdom. "This is Cameron. He is an artist who works in a medium called Touch Drawing."

"And, last but not least… maybe smallest, but not least," Drew teased, "is Keesha. She has exceptional seeing and sensing abilities for her age and is an apprentice Earth messenger."

Keesha couldn't be more than eight years old, physically anyway. Her soul, however, feels ancient and she is extraordinary to look at. She has a mass of brown hair that literally looks like a lion's mane, olive skin and eyes with a blend of green, brown and gold. Her nose is small and adorably upturned.

Michele, being the senior Earth messenger, took the lead in welcoming us to walk with them.

"It's wonderful to have new, young energy joining us. We gather to walk each morning at the infinity path by the rejuvenation rooms. Your TD GPS or members of the community can guide you there, if you don't already know where it is. This time of year we are beginning at 8:00 am. We walk the path barefoot and in silence, tuning to the frequencies of the Earth. Don't think too hard about what you are sensing, just tune in and feel. We walk for half an hour or so and then move back here to the café to share what we have picked up." She paused, considering whether she wanted to share more, and then said, "That's enough for right now. You will learn more about the information you are picking up when we do our collective reporting in the café. See you tomorrow."

Joelle and Sage made eye contact and even though Drew had said Zander was the one who wanted to connect with her, Joelle seemed to know that it was important to talk to Sage also. No surprise, since Joelle had been the one to come into the dream with the clue. Zander was sitting right next to Sage, so he didn't feel like he was being ignored.

I got a hit from the disappointed look on Sage's face that she wanted to try and catch Trevor before he left, but he was headed out the door. She turned back to Joelle, who was waiting to speak with her.

"I have a feeling this is what you were wanting," Joelle said to Sage as she handed her a folded piece of paper.

Sage opened it, read it and with a quiet chuckle she just shook her head in amazement. "Yep," was all she said.

"I have to go open the wellness center," Joelle said, "and I would like to invite all of you to come over for a balancing session this morning. I also see you haven't had a chance to enjoy your breakfast yet, so we could make it comfortable and say 10:00."

Kai declined the invitation saying, "I feel I need to do some journaling this morning about what came up for me in the collective dreaming. I would love to do it another time."

"No problem. Is this morning a good time for the rest of you?" she checked in.

Zander, Sage and I all confirmed that would work.

"Great. See you then."

We polished off our breakfasts pretty quickly and Kai excused himself to go to the general store for a journal to capture his dream reflections. An interesting thing I noticed as I sat there was that we are among the few people in the café who ordered more than beverages.

"So how was it?" Sabrina cheerfully asked when she returned to collect our dishes.

"Better than expected, and it did seem to give me an energy boost and more clarity," I said, taking the time to really check in with my body, rather than selecting an answer from the menu of standard responses that match that question.

"I'm intrigued by something here," I continued. "I haven't really seen many people eating around the center and for how active it is all day, there aren't a lot of food places. Why is that?"

Sabrina set the tray of dishes on an expandable rack for trays on the side of our booth.

"Basically, because this dimensional plane functions at a higher frequency, we are able to be charged more directly from sources like the sun. When people do choose to eat, it is more for the pleasure of experiencing the tastes, textures and energies of the food. Our bodies are very efficient at deriving value from what we consume. We also need less food because what we eat has a very high life force, different than when food was overly processed, zapped, genetically modified and toxic with chemicals.

Food is still a way that we nurture each other, but it is not the primary focal point for connecting socially. As you've seen, there are so many ways to engage with each other creatively that there isn't so much inner space we are trying to fill with food.

There is also a relationship with the Earth that feeds us, and that's why we have so many gardens, both food and ornamental. We are actually being nourished and healed physically by the balancing frequencies of the Earth, such as the Schumann resonance, when we have our hands in the soil."

"Thanks for that explanation. It makes perfect sense," I said.

Sage and Zander were ready to go and slid out of the booth, thanking Sabrina for everything.

"I'll catch up with you two at the wellness center, if that's okay. I want to check in with Drew about something before I leave here and then grab a shower and change my clothes back at my room before the balancing session," I suggested.

"That works for me," Sage replied. "What about you, Zander?"

He simply nodded, yes, and they headed out.

Drew was just wrapping up a conversation with someone at the front of the café, when he saw me head toward the front door and he motioned for me to hang on a minute.

When Drew was complete he came over and said, "Chrysalis, I'm glad I got a chance to talk to you one-on-one. When I shared my dream this morning, I had the sense that you were the one who was telling stories at the café. Did that resonate with you at all when I said it?"

"I do make up stories about people in my head. It's sort of a way I amuse myself."

"In the dream, there was an element of light entertainment with creating the stories for people on the spot and then seeing how accurate they are, but there's more to it," Drew said trying to tease out the deeper meaning of what he had envisioned. "Bear with me for a minute while I play with this and see where it wants to go. I know when people seek out psychics, or other kinds of energy readers, they usually want someone to confirm something positive about them… they want to know the future holds a desired potential. It often gives them something to hold on to in darker times. The stories we tell about each other are powerful, and it is ground we should hold sacred if we want to bring our unrealized potential forward.

Although it appears that the challenges you face in your time-space reality have all been resolved, as evidenced in the **future** experienced here, this is actually a **parallel** occurrence. They are intertwined in a way your linear mind can't understand, and we must all be true to playing out our stories with the highest integrity. In other words, we've all agreed to show up and be in the game. And, it's only engaging when we don't know the outcome."

A deep chill ran through my body and I couldn't speak. Drew let me take it in and then continued.

"Many of the interdimensional visitors from different time-space realities, in various game groupings, hang out at the café. Locals come here as well. What would you say about arranging a night to play with the storytelling idea, just to see how it flies?"

"I don't know if I could do it, if people were expecting something really profound. You just said that seeing a bright possibility can give someone something to hold on to in darker times. Do people really experience that kind of thing here?"

"Not to the same degree that they do in your dimension but, even in the best of circumstances, people can forget the greater truth of who they are. The difference here is that the collective field is much more supportive of **re-membering**. Thoughts and emotions have a magnetic quality and they stick to those that are similar. That's why when there is a predominance of negative thinking it is harder to break free of it. So much is perceptual and we know we have the power to change the lens we are looking through. I wouldn't worry about doing it 'right.' Just play with it in the same way you do naturally in your head. There would be no suggestion in the way we promote it that this is 'serious.' But when a **truth** slips through that registers in a powerful way, it can be **life changing**."

"Okay, I'll think about it. Right now I have to get over to the wellness center to meet Sage and Zander, so I'll come back later to talk about when you were thinking of doing it."

"Sounds good."

There is so much information coming in so fast but, oddly, it doesn't feel like a lot to process. It's different from being absorbed in thought and having my field of perception narrow. Instead, there is an expansion and a heightened sensory awareness that is only available when I find my way to stillness. I'm noticing that in that quiet, present state things become known without thinking. It also transforms each scene from something like the simple 2-dimensional line drawings of the original Disney animation to 3-dimensional images coming out of the screen. My body feels absolutely electric with excitement, wonder and amazement at it all.

As I made my way along the path to my room, I ran into Luna on her way to the community center. She is an interesting combination of voluptuous, seductive young woman with the face of a sweet little girl cuddling a teddy bear. It definitely gets her noticed.

As soon as I saw her, I realized she would have gotten Will's card sooner if I had held on to it, rather than giving it to Sage, as Kai suggested. I know he was trying to be efficient in the way that seemed most logical. I actually did feel that Will handed it to me for a reason, but I had discounted it. Then I reflected on one of the guidelines for the game Max went over yesterday, **trust your feelings over logic**.

"Hey Luna, there was a clue we received from an interesting guy at the café this morning, which seemed to be for you. He said his name was Will and then he said, "When the moon is beginning to get full, have **her** come and see me. The butterfly in the observatory can show her the way." He gave me his card, but I gave it to Sage thinking you might see her sooner. We were trying to determine who the clue was for, and we agreed that the moon Will referred to as **her** was you. What I hadn't put together until now was, I am supposed to go with you when you meet with him, because of the reference to the butterfly in the observatory showing the way. Anyway, Sage has the card he gave me and I don't really know what it says. You'll have to get it when you see her. Will you let me know what the card says when you get it?"

"Ya, for sure. Now I'm really curious. I'm gonna send Sage a text so we can make a plan to rendezvous and I can get it from her," Luna said.

"I'd love to check in more on your experience here so far, but I have to change and get over to the wellness center," I explained. "Maybe we can spend some time together when we connect around whatever this clue is about…ya?"

"Ya, we can do that. Enjoy the wellness center."

"I'm sure I will. Have fun with your explorations!"

I didn't take long changing and getting back over to the wellness center. The thought of some downtime in a balancing session was sounding really good. As I entered the building, I saw Sage and Zander checking out some of the interesting exercise equipment in the front section.

Joelle saw me come in and said, "Great! Now that you are all here, let me give you a quick tour around the center and then I will set you all up in the balance wheel.

Basically, everything here is geared toward maintaining balance. By being highly tuned to our internal feedback systems and putting attention on what creates wellness, we have very little illness in the way you think of it. This center is an optimal combination of advanced exercise technologies for the most efficient and enjoyable workouts; a live juice bar for the high-vibration nutritional support that some body types still require; and the balance wheel for subtle energy integration. For us it's like keeping the car well maintained rather than having to do mechanical overhauls—much more satisfying," she said smiling.

Joelle pointed out each of the sections, as we made the loop around the center, the whole of which was no bigger than a decent sized athletic club. Then we came to a door that divided the high energy activity portion of the center from the dimly lit, womblike chamber that we entered. I could tell this was Joelle's favorite part of the center as she described it with the pride of a mother showing pictures of her baby.

"This wheel consists of seven individual sections facing the central atrium. The atrium is a smaller version of what is in the main part of the community center. The near-ceiling-height plants and water features have full spectrum spotlights focused inward with just enough wattage to keep the plants healthy, while still maintaining the relaxing and nurturing ambience of the room. The foliage in the center of the wheel is dense enough to create privacy between the individual chambers.

The divider walls for the sectionals are lunar LCD glass that continually changes hues, providing an element of color therapy. Different painters in the community created mural-size paintings with their vision of the most beautiful world they could imagine. Each of the paintings were transferred as giclee prints onto a photo laminate and were then adhered to the individual panels of glass. The glass frames the murals in softly changing hues and the murals create privacy between the pods.

Inside each pod is a zero gravity chair with headphones and embedded transducers for a whole-body vibrational experience. You can select from classical music, binaural beats, guided meditations, or other sound healing options. Additionally, there is an option of light therapy by laying this special blanket over you. It is an array of one thousand near infrared and other wave lengths of red and blue LED light diodes laid into a blend of fibers for strength and comfortable weight and feel on the skin.

The preprogrammed frequency programs support each of the body systems, such as the endocrine and hormonal, digestive, lymphatic, circulatory, connective tissue, brain, etc.," Joelle wrapped up.

Before coming here, I was a little concerned that the balance wheel might be too much sensory stimulation for Zander, until I realized that this is what he had drawn after the collective dreaming. Sage seemed to have had the same "aha" as we all looked at each other, recognizing the perfection of our being here with Zander.

Joelle had tuned into our concerns on behalf of Zander and she offered, "The balance wheel should feel very soothing and it will help make incongruent frequencies congruent, which is sort of a smoothing out of static signals so that the body can get clear information.

We now know that what you referred to as autism has a connection to dysregulation of oxytocin. As you may know, oxytocin is the hormone and neurotransmitter that helps us bond and be able to give and accept touch. Connections with imbalances in the stomach will also start to come to the forefront in your time. For example, the perception had always been that serotonin was produced in the brain, when in fact 80% is produced in the stomach.

The way we balance stress here, which is at the heart of all illness, is to let the incredible, innate intelligence of the body use the frequencies it needs and ignore the rest. We respect that all things are connected in ways that we will never fully understand. The 'supreme intelligence' has breathed itself into every cell and the mind can dance with that larger awareness, but was never intended to lead.

Individuals like Zander, were seen as dysfunctional and having special needs. But, really they are high sensory beings who are barometers for what is too staticky in your world. They have come to help people of your time learn another way."

"Can I get in?" Zander asked eagerly, pointing to the balance wheel pods.

"Absolutely!" Joelle affirmed. "Please choose your pods and I'll get you all started. It's best if you are wearing light-transparent clothing for the light therapy. The clothing you received upon arrival, like what Zander has on, is designed for that. Each pod has a robe made of that material, if you would like to change in to that. There is a shield that will come up from the floor when you enter the pod that will give you privacy. Please put your TDs on silent and place them on the bench inside the pod for your belongings. The session will be a half hour. You may fall asleep, so a very gentle bell will sound at the end. Feel free to take your time reorienting to your body when the session is over."

The balancing treatment seemed to be over in a few minutes because I had gone out so quickly and so deeply. Just as it started, I do remember seeing similar geometric patterns to those that flashed through my mind in the canyon when I met Trevor. This time though, the information didn't seem overwhelming. It's all beginning to feel familiar, and my mind is relaxing with trying to make sense of it. It feels like I'm being rewired and integration is happening without my trying. It's not something I could really explain to anyone.

After we had all re-emerged from our journeys in the wheel, each of us was glowing and I could feel Zander's presence in a way that was distinctly different. When we turned the TDs back onto notification mode, Zander had a message from Cameron.

"Would you like to meet me at the art space for Touch Drawing? It could be a good way to express some of what you've just experienced."

"That's timely," Joelle commented, as if she was as happily surprised by the synchronicity as we were.

Zander texted him back, "Great! Are you there now?"

"Yes, and I have some munchies if you're hungry. See you soon."

Sage and I looked at each other in amazement, and she asked Zander, "Are you good to get there by yourself?"

He hesitated for a moment and then said, "Yes."

Joelle offered, "I can make that really easy for you by transferring Cameron's contact information into your TD. I have all of the Earth messengers stored."

She located Cameron in her directory and then said to Zander, "Press the telecom icon on your TD and then just hold it next to mine and it will transfer. When you ask the GPS to locate Cameron, it will get you to the right pod and then indicate where he is in the space."

"Have a great time, Zander," I said like a big sister proud of her little brother going off to school on his first big day, although Zander is way taller than me. "Call one of us if you need anything."

"So what's in store for the two of you this afternoon?" Joelle warmly inquired.

"I'm going to the labyrinth at 2:00," Sage said, as if making a passing comment that she didn't really want to give more information about.

I picked up the vibe and didn't want to nose into her business. It seemed like kind of a knee-jerk protective reaction. I can relate, because I still find myself having some of those here. However, as Drew pointed out earlier in the café, they seem to quickly pass without a similar thought to attach to.

Anyway, I was curious about where the labyrinth was. I answered Joelle's question about my plans, saying, "I think I'll just do some general exploration of the center and maybe check out the labyrinth, **later** this afternoon." I wanted to make it clear to Sage that I wasn't going to show up there when she was having her personal time.

"Sorry for being so dodgy," Sage confessed sheepishly. "I just have a tendency to hold some things close to the chest, particularly when it comes to sacred time and ritual that I don't want to share with others. I'm actually meeting Trevor to go out to the third mesa in the canyon."

"Cool," I said, as I flashed on Joelle giving Sage a note at the café this morning after the introductions with the Earth messengers.

I was still thinking about Drew's suggestion that I tell stories at the café. So maybe I'll hang out in the community center this afternoon and see how it feels to play with creating stories about the people I observe there.

Before Sage and I headed off in our separate directions, I remembered the card she had from Will to give to Luna. Since Sage is heading out to the canyon this afternoon, I'm thinkin I can get it to Luna sooner. Plus, I wanted to read it, since I realized I'm supposed to be a part of that loop.

Sage must have picked up on my thought because she said, "Luna's going to be at the intergenerational learning center at 1:00 and I was going to meet her there to give her the card. If you're going to be hanging around the center anyway, could you do it?"

I smiled, loving the way the pieces fall together so easily here, "Sure!"

She handed me the card and I looked at it.

Will Ing
Master Weaver

_____

_____

_____

_____

_____   _____

_____

CHAPTER 11

Resource-ful

I entered the intergenerational learning center and saw Luna seated at a narrow, café-type counter, looking at a micro-thin computer screen that was flush with the wall in front of her. She was reaching up to scroll across the wall-mounted screen and, as I got closer, the sleeveless cotton top she was wearing made it easy to see her bare arm. My eye went directly to a tattoo on the underside of her right wrist. It was small, and not something I would have paid much attention to, if I hadn't just seen it. Luna must have found my fascination with it odd, especially given how it had momentarily short circuited my social skills.

Luna looked down at the tattoo on her arm and then back at me and said, "What's up, Chrysalis?"

"Hey, sorry," I stammered. "Your tattoo threw me off..."

"Why's that?" she asked curiously.

I pulled out Will's card and showed it to her.

"Is that the card you told me about on the path this morning?" she said with some confusion, thinking that Sage was meeting her here to deliver it.

"Ya, Sage had an invitation to go to the canyon with Trevor this afternoon, so she asked if I could get it to you."

"What does this symbol mean?" I asked pointing to the tattoo, which matched what was on Will's card.

"It's a hexagram from the *I Ching*… the 13th hexagram to be exact. It means 'fellowship with men.' An interpretation of it that I found on the Internet, which I really resonate with, is:

> 'I come out of black stillness
> like the flowers returning to new life.
> I am one of many
> as we reach to join in community.
> We embody strength in character
> when no one is the authority.
>
> Our ideas are made brilliant by joining the flames
> of our inner visions as we share
> the experience of love within friendship.'"

"Wow! That is so cool," I said, excited by how pieces of the clue were being revealed.

"Remind me again about what Will said when he gave you the card this morning," Luna requested.

"Okay, so after telling us that relationship was more important than automation, he handed me the card and said, 'When the moon is beginning to get full, have **her** come and see me. The butterfly in the observatory can show her the way.'"

Luna's interest was definitely piqued and she said, "So what do you make of that?"

"Well, those of us at the table when the clue came figured that the moon he was referring to as **her** must be you. That's the only part we paid attention to at that time. Later, I remembered a blue butterfly that came into the observatory last night at the collective dreaming. Maybe it literally means **that** butterfly will appear again to guide you, but I think it could also mean me."

"So, what's your sense of 'when the moon is beginning to get full,' and where is it you think you're supposed to guide me?" Luna continued with her exploration.

"I'm not sure about the when, but I have a feeling the where is the textile center, since Will was dressed in nice clothes and his card says, Master Weaver."

"Did you come to the intergenerational center just to meet Sage and pick up the card, or are you planning to do something else here?" I asked, wondering if there might be a tie-in with Will's clue and why she was here.

"I signed up to meet with someone about how the monetary system works, because I came from a part of the country that was experiencing great poverty as a result of long-term drought and a dying meat packing industry, which was the basis of the economy. There was also no relief being offered by government agencies. Part of my question in the game is how we can remake ourselves from seemingly nothing. The way things work here fascinates me, particularly the monetary system."

"I'd definitely like to know more about that too, although I don't think it has anything to do with Will's clue," I chimed in. "Mind if I join you?"

"I don't see why not, and I'm guessing they may even be expecting you, given how serendipitous everything is here," Luna remarked. "I think the instructor should be here soon."

Luna took a seat on a child-size chair, in what is probably a kid's story circle just to the left of the entrance. I just hovered in the area near her. Then a distinguished, white haired Polynesian man came from the back of the learning center. He was proud and noble looking... a large, solidly built man with a casual shirt and pants and no shoes. He looked more like someone to take us out on a backcountry wilderness tour than an expert on monetary systems; but then he is probably closer to the roots of this system than any white, business-clad economist.

With one of the broadest, most welcoming smiles I've ever seen, he approached us and said, "I'm Misa. Are you the ones who are here to learn about our monetary system?"

We both nodded and introduced ourselves to him.

"Can we take a walk?" he asked.

I think we were both somewhat surprised, and at the same time delighted that this wasn't going to be a boring PowerPoint type lecture. When Joelle had brought me by here on the introductory tour, I do remember her saying that learning happens here through bringing the subject matter alive for the student. So, without hesitation we both said, "Ya!"

We headed out away from the center toward an arroyo dotted by pinon pine, cactus, sage, and swaths of wildflowers. The sun was warm and the air buzzing with various insects and birdsong.

We walked for probably five minutes before Misa queried, "What's here?"

I wasn't quite sure what type of answer he was looking for and Luna seemed equally perplexed.

Luna offered, "A desert? Plants... rocks... birds... insects..."

"Yes, a living system. Does this system change or become threatened based on the fluctuations in the money system?"

It was an interesting question, but it seemed rhetorical, and we shook our heads, no, as he continued.

"Does an apple tree quit producing apples because there aren't enough people wanting them, or with enough money to buy them? No, it just does what it does and continues to produce, and what doesn't get used goes back into the system. Additionally, apple trees don't have to make sure they have enough money in the bank to take nutrients from the soil... Who is monitoring the exchange of energy in this eco-system?... No one."

Luna continued her exchange with Misa, "Until someone identifies a part of it as resources."

"Excellent," Misa said. "And, how did they come to claim ownership of it and the right to sell it for a value they determined?"

"By buying it?" Luna said tentatively, knowing there was more to the answer.

"That's one possibility, but I want you to go back farther. How is it that people began to claim ownership of what was given freely and here for all equally?" Misa continued to probe.

"Through wars... conquest and exploitation for greed and power," I jumped in. "And, that included enslaving people as resources to be owned."

"Greed and power are a part of it, but beneath it was fear that there wasn't enough and that they wouldn't get their share. And, as it regards owning other humans, it was the fear of what was different, especially anything 'dark' was seen as a force that needed to be kept in check. Those who were strong and intelligent enough to instill fear in others did so in order to create a system of control. I don't really want to focus on that further, other than to say that fear and lack was what turned a basic medium for exchange of energy into a system that gave a small percentage of people the authority over how the resources would be allocated or earned. The point is that humans came to accept that everything that exists on the planet belongs to someone, and that those who **own** it have the right to dictate how it is used.

In general, people from your time believed that they had to **earn** the right to the basic necessities of life. When you are children, your parents earn it for you, if they are able. As adults you are expected to work, often at jobs you don't like so you can earn sufficient money to meet your needs. The indoctrination to meeting the requirements of those in control of the resources was so thorough, that the acceptance of it was on the level of it becoming a universal truth. In other words, you were convinced that you must play by the rules, if you wanted to have access to what you needed to succeed in the system. Those rules were also thought to be fixed and unchangeable."

"I'll buy that," I said, not realizing how I was playing right into Misa's hand.

"Interesting the language you chose, which reflects how everything has been commoditized and given a value. An idea that makes sense becomes something you are willing to **buy**. Have any of you ever said something like, 'I want to make myself of value,' as if your beingness isn't enough? Ideas harvested from the collective field were claimed exclusively and patented so they could be sold. Again, out of fear that someone would steal the idea and you would be left with nothing. Even intangibles such as love became something you had to earn."

"When did the money system we know change?" Luna asked curiously.

"There was a period of transition, because there was so much acceptance of it as some type of absolute truth. When the beginning suggestions of a new system were presented, it was like telling people the air was going to be taken away. Actually, before the transition to something entirely new, your system was dependent on debt because it was no longer backed by anything of value. The more debt, the more money was printed. It was all just a matter of computer entries. It was only when the system finally collapsed under its own unsustainable weight that something else became possible. New systems, including the one we use, were in place with the bugs worked out by 2030.

In our system there is definitely exchange, but the basis of it is completely different. We simply meter energy and keep human judgment out of the valuing of that. We also create security for people with the basic credit. The initial concern, which was a bleed-through from your system, was that people would be unmotivated to do anything, but we have found that to be far from true. When people feel secure, and grateful for the freedom to explore what really matters to them, the impulse is to 'pay it forward.' Also inherent in our system is the understanding that flow keeps things dynamic and vital. Hording out of fear that you won't have what you need leads to stagnation."

At this point, I felt the impulse to comment on what Misa was saying. "I don't know what the houses here are like inside, but from the outside they seem pretty small and I'm guessin that people don't have a whole lot of stuff, at least not compared to what I am used to."

Misa seemed to appreciate the transition from monologue back to dialogue.

"You're right, because one of the requirements of your economic system was continual growth. That meant that people had to be **sold** on the idea that they weren't enough without some product or service. Also, planned obsolescence and cheap goods kept consumption up,

137

so a lot more resources got used and people had a lot more 'stuff.' Because profit was a key component to making the system work, what people had to pay in exchange for the products they purchased was far greater than what it actually cost to produce them."

"So, you just said that flow keeps things dynamic and hording creates stagnation. I'm curious how that's different from keeping money flowing with buying products to sustain a strong economy?" I queried, looping back for clarification.

"There are some essential differences," Misa explained. "In the continual growth model, no importance is given to renewal of the Earth's resources. It's an extraction-based process that creates imbalance. The flow of money is largely for external goods, which tend to lose their first blush of promised happiness quickly. The continual growth model, based on consumption, leads to overall, cumulative depletion on all levels.

Here, energy and resources are generated more than depleted, because what we value is personal growth and wellbeing, which comes from expressing our creativity, enjoying cultural experiences, and other ways of deepening our connections with one another. We also make it a priority to replenish the physical resources we do use. In nature there is always a period of rest and renewal, never continual growth."

"This is exactly the conversation I wanted to have," Luna said in acknowledgment of Misa. "So what are the basics that people have to pay for through their transaction accounts?"

"They pay for the materials for their homes, which are quite modest; a small amount of food; clothing; transport vehicles, if they want one, but they can easily get by using the teleportation system, which is equivalent to buying a bus pass; TDs; and any other personal electronic devices. Additionally, we share in the building cost of the community center. We also have replicators in the different artisan pods, which are a further development of the 3D printers that came into use in your time for manufacturing things at a very low cost. Other than that it's pretty much what people do for personal enrichment and entertainment."

"What about power, water, telecommunication service and healthcare?" Luna continued.

"When the profit and control piece got released, so did the free energy technologies. Our power source is a matter-antimatter plasma reactor that is very small and efficient. Having free energy radically decreased the production cost of our goods.

Additionally, transportation charges that added a significant amount to the cost of both manufactured goods, delivery of fossil fuel and distributed power became obsolete with new, local power sources and the teleportation system. At the same time, toxic by-products of the old transportation system and the need for expensive cleanups were eliminated. This also positively impacted how much people had to spend on healthcare.

Small cubes, called femtocells, replaced cell towers and enhanced the signal power of our optical fiber network, which consists of highly transparent strands of glass that transmit light signals over long distances. The cost continues to come down with the improvements in technology.

We still pay for water, but we utilize permaculture design for the capturing and recycling of water. You may have seen the solar sewage walls that look like greenhouses for purifying grey and even black water. The toilets we use also do some pre-purification. Additionally, our gardens are planted with biointensive agriculture techniques to enhance the water retaining capacity of the soil. Basically, it becomes a living sponge. In the desert, every bit of mindfulness about the use of and reclaiming of water is important.

As far as healthcare costs go, we went back to the ancient Chinese medicine practice of paying our physicians to keep us well. Also, the move to more subtle energy modalities, which honor that we are more energy than dense matter, costs much less than invasive procedures to deal with extreme imbalance. The old system was fear-based and one that generated a lot of profit from illness. Our stress level here is imperceptible compared to what you came from. Everything here is geared to support life, enrichment and enjoyment.

Luna was obviously animated by the concepts. "This is so exciting! I'm trying to envision how to help my community get to this from where it is currently."

Misa assured her, "Remember that people are the greatest resource in your community! The collective imagination and commitment to each other will bring it all together.

Our community center operates smoothly because people want to be in relationship with each other and with the Earth. People are filled on many levels when they come to the center and participate. **Everyone** has unique gifts and we appreciate all of them, no matter how simple. The joy of giving and co-creating feeds everyone.

People you might think would have challenges meeting their basic needs, because of physical impediments, are resource-ful and easily generate credits in their transaction accounts. Some of the most inspiring people in history were categorized as having disabilities, but they taught us how to soar without wings. That's worth a lot.

You don't need to wait to have a monetary system like this. It is actually the way the universe works, so have faith and it will be so."

"Misa, if this is the way the universe actually works then why are so many good people who help each other struggling to make ends meet in our time?" Luna reflected.

"Have there been times when you stopped yourself from the impulse to help someone because you felt you didn't have the money to do it? Well in our system, stopping yourself from that act of caring would result in an energy debit in your account. Just the fear of not having enough is a slow drain on your transaction account and becomes a self-fulfilling prophecy, if you don't catch it. If everyone could **genuinely** believe there is enough, and that they are worthy to receive the abundance that is waiting for them, it would all start to change.

So, the short answer to your question is, because people didn't believe it could be different. Unfortunately, the predominant impulse of your time was fear and lack, and that's the energy that created the reality you find yourselves in. When you live from joy and doing the things you love, and respond to the impulse to give, your transaction account fills up with credits. So, as you've seen this is a much kinder and happier world," Misa concluded, as he stood taking in the beautiful expanse.

When the urge moved, we began walking back to the center in silence... the sun bleached day giving way to color and a sense of settling. Just before we got to the learning center, Misa said, "I'm going to head off in this direction," indicating the nearby housing section, where I assumed his home was.

"Thank you, Misa. That was the best economics lesson I've ever had and it was so helpful," Luna offered.

"Ya, Misa, I hope we'll have a chance to see you again while we're here," I added.

"Me too. You've both been great," Misa said with the same warm smile he greeted us with.

Then Luna and I looked at each other like, what next?

"I'm feeling like free-formin it a bit," I said, realizing how this day had been packed with one thing after another, and I was ready for some space out and people watching time. "How 'bout if we reconnect tomorrow to get a sense of when the right time is to find Will and to see what that's about?"

Luna agreed. "I don't feel like I'm 'getting full,' I feel like **I am full**, so maybe we missed the intended rendezvous with Will. I hope not. I'll think about what else that could mean and also pay attention for any new information."

"I'm walking with the Earth messengers in the morning. I'll connect with you after that," I said as I headed to find a place to chill and people watch in the center.

It feels like so much is happening so fast and I appreciate the connections that are being made so easily with the others from the game group and the community. Then I thought about Zander and how I agreed to help him navigate the space. I realized the last time I saw him was when he went off to Touch Drawing with Cameron earlier today.

I pulled out my TD, pressed the GPS icon and asked, "Where's Zander?" It located him back in his guestroom and I sent a quick text, "Doing okay? Need anything?"

His reply came back, "Watching movies. See you in the morning."

I realized that I would be with the Earth messengers in the morning and couldn't hang with him, so I shot a text back. "Can't come for you til later in the AM."

"Cameron is comin to get me."

Hmm, I know Cameron will be walking with us in the morning, so I'm not sure what Zander meant, but I won't worry about it since it seems like it's all cool.

I thought about how handy these devices are when you want to find someone, and at the same time how that could be an annoyance, if you wanted to make yourself invisible. I suppose you could just leave your TD somewhere, but then that would also mean not having access to your vehicle, telecommunications, or anything you needed to buy.

The young woman sitting next to me on the bench in the central atrium picked up on my thought and timidly said, "You do have the right to put it on 'do not disturb' mode. The TDs are only meant to be useful, not invasive."

I chuckled, thinking to myself, what difference does it make if I put the TD on 'do not disturb' when the whole bloody field is transparent?

"It can be hard to adjust to, since your default when you first get here is fear and protecting yourself. By the way, did you know that the moon will start getting full tomorrow at noon?" she happened to mention as she stood, smiled at me and walked away.

"No I didn't, but I do now! Thank you very much!"

I shot off a quick text to Luna: "Clue surfaced. Moon getting full @ noon tomorrow. C U @ textile center."

When Zander mentioned the movie it sounded pretty good, and so does kickin off these cowboy boots and climbing into my cushy-bed-slash-sensurround theater. Just as I got up from the bench and turned to head in that direction, I saw Trevor and Sage come into the center after being at the canyon for the afternoon. They hugged goodbye, then Sage continued on to the café and Trevor came toward me. There is just something about him that is so familiar and so comfortable. He has the kind of strong, yet gentle presence that just makes me want to curl up in his lap and have him stroke my hair.

"Hey Chrysalis, I'm glad I ran into you. I was thinking about you today and wanted to thank you again for stepping in with Zander the day of the orientation when I had to rush off. How's he doing anyway?"

"Good, I think. He's in his room watching a movie right now, if you want to check in with him."

"Maybe I will… So, how are you adjusting?" he asked, wrapping me energetically with the warmth I had just been imagining.

"Awesome. This is an amazing place… a little overwhelming, but amazing. This whole game thing is pretty mind-boggling too. Is it against the rules to ask how you all generate the clues?"

He smiled in a really cute way of biting his lower lip, like he was about to give away the magic trick. "No, it's not against the rules because there really aren't any rules. There's also no set plan. Because of the way things function here, we just tune into someone's question and go with our intuition and imagination and have fun playing. We actually are as much in the game as you are. I believe the 'divine intelligence' loves to play as much as we do. I also think that in a way 'spirit' wants to realize its ever evolving potential in us, as us and through us."

"What do you mean?" I asked, trying to grok the whole concept.

"Well, we might give a clue without exactly knowing how it will play out. It's kind of like improv comedy, if you're familiar with that. We trust each other to pick up on what we throw out and to make it work. And then of course, the universe is also on board connecting all the clues in much better ways than we could have planned. Those are the synchronicities that **everyone** involved is blown away by. So, basically, we just show up and get to be a part of the magic."

"Wow, it's amazing that you can just **trust** it to work so consistently... and it does. I think your telling me that just added to my sense of wonder and appreciation. Anyway, you've probably had a full day and I was just going to catch a movie myself."

"Sounds good... I'll see you in the morning then," he said as he put his arm around my shoulder and gave me a squeeze, and I laid my head against his heart with my arms wrapped around his waist. I didn't want him to let go, but he did. It was okay though, because I knew how to find him again.

CHAPTER 12

Deep Listening

I woke up with my heart racing because something was chasing me. It felt like something dark and old. As I lay there wet with anxious perspiration, I heard, "Go back into the dream and meet it." I did and, when I turned unafraid and faced it, it dissolved. The voiceless voice then said, "What dream do you want to dream now?"

I opened my eyes and tried to orient myself to where I was… what day it was… what I was supposed to be doing. I was in a beautiful bed raised up into a ceiling dome. I could barely see the white screen that created an inner layer on the dome, blocking all visual indicators of where I was. This must be what it feels like to be a chick inside a shell.

Then I remembered that I was watching movies last night in this cozy little nest… that I am at Escalante de Luz… and that I am supposed to be walking with the Earth messengers this morning. I had no sense of what time it was because of the white screen covering the dome and I patted around on the bedding trying to locate my TD. I found it near the edge of the bed and glanced at the glowing numbers on the screen… 6:30… oh good, I had plenty of time to get to the infinity loop by 8:00.

The community center was also still waking up as I passed through on my way to the path beyond the rejuvenation rooms. The freshness of the spring air was punctuated by bits of dew gifted by the night to an otherwise sunbaked desert. The spring bloom was in its glory. I took time to savor it all, as I prepared for the listening we will do in our walking of the loop.

The others were all there when I arrived, except for Cameron. There wasn't any chatty connecting happening. Instead, there was a profound stillness and a level of reverence I had never experienced in churches. I removed my shoes, as the others had, and wiggled my toes to make sure they were all paying attention.

Then Cameron arrived with Zander and I remembered Zander's text last night that he would see me this morning. Zander was carrying art materials for drawing and Cameron directed him to a good spot to sit. No explanation was required by any of the regular walkers. They just held their inward focus.

Michele stepped onto the path first, walking slowly, like I had seen people do in walking meditation. One by one the other walkers followed, as the impulse seemed to move them, like bees darting randomly out of the hive. All walkers followed the same infinity pattern as the bees doing their work.

We were all spaced out along the path, with none walking side by side. I was following the cue of those ahead of me to touch the right hand fingertips to those of the walkers passing at the intersection point—some going out and others returning to the beginning. It reminded me of ants touching antennae and exchanging some kind of information. I also saw that people were making more than one round of the loop and, feeling like I had the basics of the process, I dropped deeper into my own sensing. I trusted that I would know when I was complete.

Today, I noticed a deep hum beneath the normal chorus of insects. Something about it made me want to keep moving and I was the last of the walkers to exit the path and return to the café, where the sharing of what was picked up happens.

As I entered the café, I saw the messengers in what I assumed was the usual spot, since it was where they were yesterday. Drew was near the front entrance. When I came in, I realized I never made it back yesterday to follow up with him on our earlier conversation.

"Hey Drew, I need to drop in over there," I said gesturing to where the walkers were seated. "Sorry I didn't get back…"

He interrupted before I could finish, "No worries. Catch me before you leave."

When I got to the table, they were passing around the picture Zander had drawn while out at the path. Cameron was sharing why he invited Zander to be part of this morning's ritual.

"When I met Zander, I got that we had something in common. After spending time together yesterday at the art center, I could see that he has precognitive gifts, which he shares through his drawing. I thought it would be interesting to see how that might contribute to our collective understanding of what we picked up walking."

As I took a seat around the large, round table, I was handed the picture and briefly glanced at it. I could see that Michele was ready to start the check-in process and I set the drawing aside to pay attention.

"Cameron, thanks for your insight about Zander. I'm sure it will prove to be valuable information," she began graciously.

"Before we get into discussing what we picked up on the path this morning, I want to give those of you who have joined us for the first time today a brief overview of why we do this.

Some time ago, it became apparent that the imbalances in the Earth were such that natural disasters could undo the wealth of all nations and threaten life as we know it. We had stopped listening to what the Earth was saying and the relationship was falling apart. At least that was true for the 'developed' nations.

Now, there are groups of Earth messengers all over the planet who tune to the incongruent patterns. Those of you who have been to the wellness center have probably heard some of this same language, because essentially our bodies and the Earth's body function the same. When the systems of the Earth, or your body, are overly stressed there is a staticky signal. Meaning, energy isn't flowing easily. It's stuck somewhere, or there's too much pressure somewhere that is looking for a way to release.

In the same way that we compare notes on what we perceive within our community, we also share information with the global web of messengers. We use the telecommunication system to report our findings to the global network and to confirm that we are in alignment. Additionally, we recognize that the information we pick up is through a collective field, which some would refer to as the 'noosphere' or 'morphic resonance.' Tapping into that field is how we are able to sense things in other parts of the world."

Michele continued, "I am in charge of reporting our findings at the communication center. Just like news you are familiar with, we report what is locally and globally relevant.

What we call the Earth report is a broader version of a weather report and includes things like geothermal pressure, solar flares and areas of weakness, excess toxicity or other types of imbalances that require a collective focusing. For more alarming conditions, a global focusing is coordinated."

Michele must have noticed the look of concern on my face because she paused to ask, "Is there something I said that brings up fear for you, Chrysalis?"

"Well, ya, I guess hearing about all the things that could be a problem makes me feel a little helpless and vulnerable."

"That's exactly why people didn't pay attention for so long, both to the Earth and to their bodies. Back in 1936, Dr. Hans Selye introduced the term 'stress' and developed the *Selye Bar* to explain the stages the body goes through in relationship to stress. He defined three phases, with alarm being at the healthy end of the bar, progressing to adaptation and then to exhaustion at the dis-ease end. The alarm phase is nothing more than your body communicating that it is having an issue somewhere. If you tune into that, you can deal with it while it is a small disturbance. When you take a pill, or mask over that communication in some way, the body will start trying to adapt to handle it. However, when the body starts juggling too many things, the whole house of cards collapses and you have exhaustion or dis-ease, which requires more invasive and costly remedies. A simple analogy is if you don't pay attention to the fire alarm, a little smoldering fire could turn into something that burns down the whole house. So, alarms are good… Does that help you feel more open to receiving the information?"

"Ya, I guess when you put it that way it feels like it's within my power to help change it. I can see where the tendency was to want to block out information that was uncomfortable to deal with. Thanks," I said, not wanting to take any more time away from the reporting.

"You're welcome. Anyway, let's get on to checking in and, if there are more questions, I'll be happy to answer those afterwards," Michele said with both warmth and efficiency. "Who wants to start?"

Trevor led off with, "I am picking up geothermal pressure building in the Pacific Rim, with a significant blockage near Fairbanks, Alaska."

"I get that too," said Cameron, "and I'm sensing that if that isn't handled, there will be repercussions in the ley line back to the Peruvian mountains."

"Chrysalis, I noticed that you were the last to return. Do you want to share what you were perceiving?" Michele asked respectfully.

"I was just picking up an unusual humming and the energy made me feel like I wanted to keep walking."

"That indicates a level of disturbance that calls for a focused immersion to collectively move the energy. Were the rest of you sensing the same?" Michele asked as she facilitated the check-in.

All heads nodded in agreement.

"I would suggest a two-hour immersion to handle the disturbance. Are there other thoughts on that?"

Joelle said, "That feels right to me."

Michele said, "So, if there's nothing more to add, I'll go to the communication center to share our findings with the messenger network. When we do the daily news broadcast, I'll make the announcement about a local immersion to take place at 7:00 pm tonight in the performance center."

No additional input was given and Michele brought the official meeting to a close. She did add, "Luis coordinates the immersions at the performance center, so see him if you have questions."

Michele gathered her things to go get the news broadcast ready. Kai, Sage, Zander and me lingered a bit longer with Luis, and Sabrina came over to see if we needed anything in the food or beverage department. She was as cute and perky as before and it reminded me of the conversation with Will, and that I needed to be at the textile center by noon to meet Luna. I had plenty of time though and I wanted to ask Luis some questions about the immersion.

"Hey Sabrina, I'm going to be adventurous and try the *Green Goddess* today," I said proudly. She smiled approvingly, took my order and a few others and headed off.

Kai beat me to the immersion question and asked Luis, "So what exactly happens at a focusing immersion?"

"Well, there are different ways people in the community can participate. They don't actually need to come to the performance hall, but it's just a really deep, sacred space with everyone joined together. People can meditate or visualize shifting the energy, either there or in their private spaces. They can pray or chant. And, hey, maybe people like you, Zander, can create pictures of what it looks like when it's restored. Whatever people choose to do, we all do it at the same time." Luis began explaining.

I looked down at Zander's picture that was still in front of me and I saw that he had drawn a lot of heavy, black scribbly lines over what appears to be Alaska.

"Anyway, the primary thing that happens at the performance hall is a free-form ecstatic dance. The main floor of the performance center will be cleared of chairs and we will use drums, didges, and other percussion instruments amped through the transducers in the sound floor to create a conducive environment for the dancers to drop into trance. Basically, we are using our bodies as a conduit for moving the stuck energy in the Earth, since it's all connected."

"How often are immersions required?" Sage wondered in the form of words.

"About once a week, but rather than thinking of it as something that's required, we actually view it as an opportunity to come together in celebration of the Earth. We hold the vision of her as whole rather than focusing on fixing something.

I also believe that things are not always what they appear to be. Perhaps natural disasters are a way of testing the human spirit to see if we will rise to our potential for compassion and generosity, and to encourage faith that life will return all things to balance. The ancient Chinese symbol that can mean either crisis or opportunity speaks to this."

"I get it," Sage said appreciatively. "Thanks for making that distinction. I'm beginning to get a whole new sense of what it means to be a healer."

I finished my drink and left a note of appreciation for Sabrina on the table, as I stood up to go find Drew. "Hey, Luis, thanks for the explanation. I have to run now, but I hope I'll see you guys at the immersion tonight!"

Other than Zander, everyone was shaking their heads to indicate they would be there. And, even Zander seemed to be considering it. I was glad to see him feeling confident enough to start venturing out of his comfort zone. Before I left the table I whispered to him, "Seems like you got something out of the balance wheel yesterday. Are you going to go back?"

"Ya," he said, feeling encouraged.

"Text me if you need anything, okay? It will be cool if you come tonight and draw, as you pick up on the energy there."

"Ya, maybe… but I'm a little shy and socially awkward, in case you haven't noticed."

"That's why I love free-form dance… it's just about feeling good moving your body. No one is checking anyone else out or critiquing them. Anyway, if it's in the flow, I'll see you there."

I glanced around the café to see if I could locate Drew and when I didn't spot him, I went to the patio area outside. He was sitting there soaking up a bit of the morning sun that was just right this time of year. His eyes were closed and I quietly said, "Knock, knock."

He playfully responded, "Who's there?"

"Soon-to-be…"

With his eyes still closed he continued to play along, "Soon-to-be what?"

"Soon to be appearing at the café!"

"Cool, you decided to do it," he said as he glanced sideways at me through a squinted eye.

"Ya, I guess, but can you tell me more about how you think this will happen?"

"Well, I thought we would use the stage and have a spotlight on you with everyone's attention directed expectantly at you," he said with a smirk that I couldn't clearly read.

He must have picked up on my concern because he quickly added, "No, really, we'll tuck you back in a corner like a mysterious fortune teller. People can come for their own private playtime with you. It will all be in a light, good-hearted spirit. I think the less serious you are about it, the more accurate you might be."

"Okay, so when do we do this?" I asked.

"How 'bout tomorrow night at 7:00, since tonight's the immersion?"

"It's a deal… see you then… unless I see you at the immersion."

"Oh ya, I wouldn't miss it for anything."

"Awesome! See you there..." I said as I headed in the direction of the re-use trading hub to find something cool to dance in tonight.

On my way there, my TD beeped and I could see a notice streaming across the bottom about tonight's immersion. I knew it wasn't just a personal notification because I heard beeps all around me. My expectations around it were certainly building.

I was shuffling through the racks of skirts and tops looking for the right combination of comfortable, flowy, arty and sassy when I saw Cali come in. We hadn't really connected yet. She is older, like Kai, maybe twenty. She has an air of confidence that makes me feel a little intimidated. People like her represented the face of beauty that I was made to feel less than... long blond hair, blue eyes and a sparkling white smile. She moves like a powerful cheetah with its sleek, agile exquisiteness.

"Hey Chrysalis," she said warmly when she looked up and saw me, as our fingers reached the same section on the rack. "I knew I would find a treasure here!"

Instantly, any sense of her not being able to relate to me melted. Her genuine warmth was disarming and I put down the mental sword used to defend my worth, and hoped that it would soon be fully decommissioned. "You seem like you are looking for something particular," I said.

"Ya, I guess. I think what you are picking up on is that I am a little preoccupied after the journey I was on this morning in the game. Shopping is sort of a meditation that helps me integrate," she said with a chuckle.

"**Journey** sounds like you traveled somewhere. Or, are you meaning some kind of inner journey?"

"I'd have to say both. A woman in the community named Ariel and I teleported to different places on the planet that were badly scarred by things like strip mining and clear-cutting. We ended up at a place called the tar sands in Canada where they did oil extraction. Ariel showed me pictures of what those places used to look like and what they have been transformed into. Some have been naturally reclaimed by the Earth and there are others that humans brought their loving and respectful creativity to. These are now shrines and sacred places to worship the amazing regenerative, life-giving force of the Earth. The original beauty isn't there, but a new and profound beauty has emerged."

Cali paused for a moment and then, as if she was still looking at the places she and Ariel had visited, she shared, "Ariel said people here don't turn away from what's difficult to look at—that it is waiting for us to find its beauty again. They also don't forget what has happened, because it makes them appreciative of what is here now as a result of the choices they and those before them participated in making."

"Are you some kind of environmental activist?… I mean, I'm curious about what the question is that you came with," I ask tentatively, not sure if I was trespassing in raw territory.

"No, I'm not exactly an environmental activist, but it's hard to leave that out of the conversation altogether since our bodies mirror what is happening with the Earth," she said as she unlaced the loose, peasant-type blouse she had on and pulled it back to reveal a sheer lace camisole that had no purpose other than to cover scars.

"Breast cancer?" I asked, feeling tenderness that wanted to reach for her through my eyes.

She nodded. "You asked about my question… It is, 'How do I empower young women and redefine beauty?' We get interesting gifts sometime as the way we are called to our work."

We stood for a moment in silence, and all I could think was that she wore her truth beautifully. Then it occurred to me that she may not be aware of the immersion tonight.

"Cali, did you hear about the immersion?"

"I saw the announcement on my TD on my way over here, but I didn't know what it was about."

"Well, it ties in perfectly with your journey today. It's a focusing in various ways to rebalance a disturbance in the Earth, which the Earth messengers picked up this morning. One option for focusing is using our bodies as a conduit for moving energy in a free-form, ecstatic dance that will be held at the performance hall at 7:00 tonight."

"Love it… I'm a dancer and I'm totally down with that. Now, I have a specific focus for shopping," she laughed again.

Something about shopping has a way of bonding females, regardless of age and cultural differences. I could have hung with Cali and had fun for much longer, but I realized I needed to head over to the textile center soon. That's another option for clothes I haven't checked yet. I should also have plenty of time before tonight to come back here, if I need to.

"Hey Cali, I hope you find something really awesome. I have to meet Luna at the textile center at noon to follow up on a clue that came for us."

"Great! Are you having fun with it?"

"Ya, and it's different than I was expecting."

"What were you expecting?"

"I guess when I heard 'game' and 'clues' I was thinking more prepackaged and trivial... you know... just for fun, and sort of predictable. This feels more like a series of synchronistic overlaps and I'm constantly blown away by what happens in those intersections."

"Ya, I know what you mean... until our next intersection..." she said appreciatively.

I scanned a couple more items before tearing myself away from the re-use center, and I noticed Cali's attention had been captured by a beautiful tattoo down another shopper's calf, past the ankle and onto the top of her foot.

CHAPTER 13

Immersion

As I approached the textile pod, I noticed that Luna was already there and she was curiously looking at something on the ground outside the entrance. The fascinating object was a skein of yarn with the loose end of it trailing into the textile center, as if it had been placed there by a mischievous child enticing a kitten to play.

When I was in front of her, Luna looked up at me and said, "What do you think... did that just roll out here accidentally?" She made a combination groan and chuckle and surmised, "I don't know this Will character yet, but my guess is this is his way of saying, Come find me."

I agreed. Luna picked the skein up to collect the thread, and as we followed it into the center, I imagined Will behind the curtain chuckling that his bait had been taken. We gathered the fine yarn carefully as it bent around corners of a space bustling with the activity of various fabric artists exploring their crafts. They all seemed oblivious to us, as the yarn finally delivered us to Will sitting contently at his loom, shuttling threads back and forth. He was dressed in the same sharp clothing as the day I met him at the café. He reminds me of Mr. Peanut, but with round, wire rim glasses instead of a monocle.

"Welcome! You're right on time," he said as he swung around to greet us.

"Oh, I'll take that," he continued, as he reached to take the skein from Luna.

He was a delightfully quirky character, as he told us about the yarn, like it was an overly adventurous child. "Oh, it gets on a roll with wanting to go out and find new inspirations to bring back to me for the weavings, and I must say it's done a fine job today!"

All of a sudden I imagined myself being a five-year-old child in rapt wonder, as some magical character had come to life to weave an enchanting story. Luna seemed to have fallen under Will's spell as well, and we gathered round the loom and made seats in the piles of fabric.

He began with a query. "What is it that each of you requires to answer your questions?"

We looked at each other drawing a blank.

"Perhaps, a deeper understanding of what it means to be in relationship and the benefits of that?" he suggested rhetorically.

"Weaving is the perfect metaphor for illustrating the importance of that… Chrysalis, you weave stories that transform… Luna you reweave a tattered community into a quilt of many colors and spin fluff into fiber that can actually clothe, and it all depends on the strength and integrity of the relationships. The relationships are on many levels—with the self, with whatever you would call God, with the Earth, with each other one-to-one and with the larger community. If any of these relationships or fibers are missing the fabric will tear.

This can be seen most obviously in nature when key elements are removed from complex ecosystems in order to suit the needs of humans, and everything begins to unravel. The reintroduction of the wolves to Yellowstone in your time-space reality was a perfect testament to this understanding, as we watched how that one element restored the whole system, including how the water flowed.

On the loom, all fibers have equal value and as the weaver and poet, Kabir, said, 'Everyone is born equal and the world knows it. It is just the cunning who say some are born high, some low.'

Kabir also compared the created universe to a textile, which the Creator has both woven on his divine loom and is intertwined with as a yarn in the fabric. I believe he would have included the nonhuman, or what might be called inanimate objects, as a part of the divine continuum.

You see, if you focus on the relationship of the parts to the whole, everything else will take care of itself. The question, as posed by an Earth-honoring culture, might be, 'Are all my relations in order?' In western industrialized civilizations the urge was to focus on one part—one thread—as if it had no relationship to anything else. The rugged individual was supposed to be superior—not weak—but one strong fiber will still break alone. One heart cell in a petri dish will die unless you place another one next to it, and you can't do that virtually," he said as he addressed Luna specifically.

And then, seemingly in more clue-speak, he said, "It takes **virtuosity** to blend many strong voices into a balanced offering that pleases the ear."

Something clicked for me with what Will shared and I interjected, "I used to prefer being alone, because I felt like most people didn't get me. Here I want to be a part of as many explorations as I can. I feel seen and affirmed by everyone. How do I hold onto that when I return to the reality I came from?"

"Remember what it feels like to be seen and affirmed and become the one who is offering that, and then see what stories you have to tell," Will remarked kindly.

I thought about the "fortune telling" at the café that I arranged with Drew, and appreciated the opportunity to strengthen my muscles with affirming people, as Will had suggested.

Will seemed content with what he had to share and he spryly concluded, "We only roll out the carpet for new arrivals. I suspect you will have no problem finding your way out... Do feel free to pop back in if there are other questions **looming** over you, or if you want to **warp** your reality!"

We were feeling the delight of our time with Will as we headed back through the textile center. Then I snapped out of my five-year-old, storytime mode and remembered that I wanted to check out the clothing options here.

"Hey, have you gotten any clothes here?" I asked Luna.

"Ya, actually I got this bodycon mini skirt here."

"Where are the things that are for sale?" I asked, looking around the center.

"At the front, on the opposite side of where we came in," she said as she pointed in that direction.

"Thanks. I want to get something special to wear for the immersion tonight. You know about it, right?"

"Ya, I was over at the community gardens earlier today with Luis learning about biointensive agriculture and permaculture design, and he told me about it," she confirmed.

"Sage also mentioned it to me when she came through the gardens on her way over to the Biomimicry Institute," Luna added. "Her room is right next to mine and we've been hanging out together at night. I don't know how much you've gotten to know her, but she is really interesting. I appreciate how she is both really intelligent and has a light, playful side to her. She attributes some of her punny, trickster nature to her Crow grandmother who was a heyoka."

"I've heard the term, but I didn't exactly know what it meant," I confessed.

"Sage said it was great to have had that influence, because the Chinese-American side of her family tended to be more linear and academic."

"I know she is also pretty tuned in energetically, because she is walking with the Earth messengers in the mornings," I noted. "So, what's the Biomimicry Institute about, and where is it? I don't remember seeing it on the tour of the community."

"It's in the first ring of buildings to the west, as you head away from the community center. It started back in 1998 with the mission to teach scientists and other innovators how to think like nature. Sage is going out on field observations with them to learn how to be present with and to see the processes of nature, so that understanding can be translated into more Earth-friendly products.

Nature creates things so elegantly using only water, room temperature and normal pressure. For example, one strand of a spider's web actually has more tensile strength than an equivalent quantity of steel. The human approach to creating products was what scientists referred to as the 'heat-beat-treat' method; in other words, using high temperatures, intense pressure, and chemical reagents, which cost more, created more waste and resulted in toxic residue. Now that people have switched to designing with nature, the Institute is

163

largely for ongoing research and certification of products as meeting their eco-friendly standards."

"So did Sage tell you what her question was for the game?" I inquired.

"Her interest is in science and innovation, particularly related to health. Her question is how to create products that are good for both people and the planet, at a cost that makes healthcare affordable rather than **giving** people a heart attack," Luna said in a tongue-in-cheek manner.

"Now I get why her being a part of visiting the wellness center with Zander and me was important. Anyway, I'm glad I'll see you tonight at the immersion. Right now I'm going to go over and look for something to wear."

I found the section at the textile center with the handmade clothing items, which artisans had for sale. I loved that every piece was a unique work of art. I chose a really beautiful, batik silk scarf with a red and orange pattern that reminded me of the surface of Jupiter. The dress that caught my attention had a similar feel to the simple shift I got when I arrived. When I tried it on it followed the natural curve of my body perfectly. It had a mid-thigh-length-layered-handkerchief hemline that flared out to make movement easy. It was pale yellow with a scoop front neckline and a deeper v-cut back that showed a hint of the tattoo on my shoulder blade. I picked up a pair of burnt orange Capri leggings, to be covered if I want to get really wild dancing.

After completing my transaction, I started heading back to my room to leave the new clothes for changing into later, but something nudged me to drop into the metalworking studio on the way. There was a section of sales items to the left of the entrance. I took a moment to admire the beautiful southwest style silver jewelry, even though it isn't my particular taste. A bolo tie with a maze etched into the metal jumped out at me. There was a man arranging pieces in the case and he noticed my fascination with the piece.

"Are you looking for a gift for someone?" he inquired.

"Uh, no..." I said, realizing that I had drifted off somewhere. "Something about that just caught my attention."

"It's a very popular Hopi symbol. One of its common representations is of a mother and child. In a broader sense, it's the connection with the Earth mother. The beginning straight center line represents the child. The surrounding maze represents the enfolding energies of the mother. Notice that the maze does not enclose the center line representing the child. This symbolizes the support of the mother, which is constantly around us, but allows us to venture out on our own.

It's the same pattern as the labyrinth on the southwest side of the center's main entrance. It reminds us that entering the community center is like being nurtured in the mother's loving womb." He concluded saying, "**Someone is waiting for you there.**"

"Thank you," was all I said as I turned and left the center. It was only a short walk to my guestroom from the metalworking studio, so I went there first to drop off the clothes.

When I arrived at the labyrinth it was late afternoon, and the softening light offered a gentler invitation to walk. Michele was there and I felt her like the great cosmic grandmother. She was offering prayers as she turned to face each direction... finishing as she moved to face me.

"I also lost someone very dear to me too soon," she said softly, and goose bumps rose on my arms in recognition of a truth I had only a vague sense of connection to. Nevertheless, I felt a lump in my throat.

"I'm not clear why I feel sadness when you say that, but it does register," I said, feeling confused.

"Our energy patterns carry unresolved blocks from one life pattern to the next. We sense that disturbance in our physical hearts sometimes more than as a clear memory. Similar experiences will continue to be drawn to us until we complete the learning," she explained.

"I remember when I arrived, Trevor, told me I had just 'changed channels' temporarily. So, why is it that I don't have clear awareness of the channel I switched from?"

"Well, if you were fully aware of what was happening in both experiences simultaneously it would be very disorienting, and also not so enjoyable. It would be like watching two different movies at the same time. Also, to help you get the fully-embodied experience of what it is to live in **this** reality, you have to leave the other one behind. If the prior reality were presented to your controlling, ego-mind as a choice when you arrived here, there's a good chance you would have defaulted to what was familiar."

"Then why are you taking me back to some experience that brings up pain?"

"To let you bring it to conscious awareness, so you can take it into the arms of the great mother. She understands the continuum of life, which both creates and yields without judgment. She will help you release the blocked emotion so that your energy will be free to flow likewise."

I was looking into her amazingly wise eyes and I felt her as my grandmother. Then her face changed and she was my mother, and it changed again until I was standing before myself.

Then Michele was the one standing before me, motioning for me to enter the maze and she said, "Love never dies. It only changes form."

As I began my journey toward the center of the maze, Michele turned to walk away and leave me with the stillness of my own process. But, before she did, she offered a quote I remembered hearing before, "Never fear the shadows. They simply mean that there's a light somewhere nearby."

A few clouds had gathered and a gentle rain began to fall. I felt my mother in the droplets, as if she wanted to make it okay for me to cry without being noticed. Indeed, as Michele had just suggested, there was light nearby because a rainbow formed joining the rust red mesas to the deep, slate blue sky. Trevor was right about the universe putting the final touches on the magic of the game.

I was headed back into the center, slightly wet but drying quickly in the dry desert air, when I turned my TD off of "do not disturb" and saw that I had a text from Luna. It related to the clue Will gave when we were with him.

Luna's text read: Am @ the comm ctr. Sign reads:

Escalante de Luz
Virtua-City Host Community
www.virtua-city.com
Virtuosity = Virtua-City. LOL. check it out!

I go on the internet and put the URL in and up pops a social networking page:

> Bring your great skills and abilities to Virtua-City to help build the cities of the future.
>
> Create a page on our virtual platform about you and what your particular interest is in establishing a deeper sense of community. On Virtua-City you can make new friends around the world and share ideas

that inspire you. The way to keep your page active on the site is by posting how you are implementing these ideas in your real communities. Also, to make the "friend" designations meaningful, we have a biannual gathering hosted by one of our member communities. During those gatherings we leave all electronic communication devices and games at the door and get to know each other in a whole new way.

Explore how the virtual can bridge to the real and vice-versa for a greater sense of connection, learning and empowerment.

I shot a quick text back to Luna: Will rocks! ☺

It was time to head back to my room to shower, change, have a bite to eat and chill for a bit before the immersion. I thought about having something from the wall automat in my room, but somehow that didn't feel right. Instead, I made my way over to the café.

I noticed a group of people, probably a little older than me, at an intimate table in the corner. I took a small table by myself nearby.

What was unique in the relationship to food here, was that the exquisitely prepared dishes were not stepchildren who went unnoticed, and for whom affection was secondary, but the delicacies were the primary focus of what was being shared. No one was mindlessly shoving food in their mouth while being completely absorbed in words about an unrelated experience. People were feeding each other as a sacrament.

As I enjoyed watching the ritual, I noticed a different server than I had seen in the café before approach the table I was sitting near with another course. When he came to my table, I expected him to take my order, but instead he said, "The people at that table want to know if you would like to join them?"

He saw my hesitation, as if I would be crashing a party and he said, "It's something we love to share."

"Okay…" I said and stood to timidly follow him over there.

He pulled the empty chair at the table out for me and said, "Enjoy!"

"Thanks for joining us, I'm Petra," stated the tall, solidly built Eastern European looking woman. "What's your name?"

"Chrysalis."

"Hey, Chrysalis, I'm River," introduced a twentysomething, average looking guy with a little goatee.

"And I'm Josh," grinned the freckled red head, who looked like he would be a lot of fun.

Petra offered a few more words of social introduction, "It's nice to have a balance at the table. Anyway, I hope it's okay with you if we don't do more social exchange during the meal. It's more of a sensory journey with the food… Do you have any food sensitivities we should know about?"

"No food sensitivities. I'll just follow your lead on the rest," I said, actually relieved that I wouldn't have to figure out what to say about myself. It was an interesting, if not edgy, experience to sit down with a group of strangers and have them start feeding me. It also felt genuinely welcoming.

It's a good thing I'm fairly adventurous with food, because there were things I didn't recognize and not talking about them made me totally open to an unbiased exploration. Some of the dishes were deceiving, looking savory but being a subtle blend of both savory and sweet. The textures were also interesting and I have to say that I have never been so aware and appreciative of what I was eating.

When the bill came, they took care of it and we all stood to go.

Josh said, "Maybe we'll see you at the immersion."

I shook my head yes, and said, "Thanks so much for including me."

There was a funnel of people from all directions headed toward the performance center. The steady drumming, and core-activating didge, created a pulse that invited movement. There were no word exchanges as people found their way out onto the floor and let their bodies start gently responding to the rhythm. Some were initially seated practicing fire breath, which I was familiar with from having taken a few yoga classes. Others began from a fetal position... reaching, stretching, rolling and exploring movement the way a baby would who is just acclimating to a body.

The room was dimly lit with a spiral of candles on what appeared to be a central altar. Over the altar, a large star icosahedron was hanging. I recognized the geometric form from somewhere and could feel it balancing the energies in the room. Waves of soft, colored light washed over the room, generated from the community's version of a disco ball. The human-generated electricity in the room was high as the collective trance state began to deepen. All I was aware of was breath and beat.

Bodies were gyrating and whirling in every direction, yet people were totally present to where they were in relationship to each other. I saw people I recognized come into the space, but I got that this was not a socializing event. I did notice that Kai and Cali had connected and were moving together in a beautiful, contact improv flow. I even spotted Zander in a more obscure corner getting familiar with what it felt like to be in his body.

There were some people who were dancing for a while, then taking breaks. For the most part, however, the intent seemed to be to pump the energy up until it couldn't go any further and then to release it. That point came about an hour and a half into the immersion. After that, I noticed people spacing themselves out on the sound floor to bask in the energy. I did the same and allowed the vibration, pulsing through the transducers, to accentuate the buzz in my body. It was ecstatic! I understand now why people here look forward to the immersions.

CHAPTER 14

Convergences

After last night's immersion, I had slept with my bed raised into the sky-dome, drinking in the delicious mystery ladled out by the Big Dipper. The moon was starting to get fuller and I felt the bathing quality of it, rather than as something that kept me awake. The peace of it all felt deeper somehow, but I suppose that had a lot to do with the space I was in when I left the collective focusing at the performance hall.

I sensed the change of dark to light through my still closed eyes. When I opened them, I gasped in wonder at the painting of the sky with peach and plum colored pancake clouds. I was hungry to begin a new day.

It will be interesting to see what the Earth messengers are picking up this morning, following the energy clearing we all participated in last night. I lowered my bed down into the main room and jumped out to get dressed and on my way.

When I arrived at the infinity loop to join the others, I no longer felt like a new comer. While they all made me feel welcomed and accepted from the beginning, I now felt worthy of their love and knew that it was genuine. Something had changed... I had changed... the tension in the Earth had changed... and it was all good!

Zander was back drawing this morning and I noticed that he had come on his own. It was wonderful to see him blossoming in a world that was ready for his beauty... where the surrounding environment nurtured rather than irritated his highly aware senses.

Today, I wasn't wondering about when it would be appropriate for me to step onto the path, I just felt in to it and went. The staticky hum from yesterday was gone, and what I picked up on more was the potent, intoxicating scent of spring blossoms being carried on a light breeze. I felt complete in two laps and headed to the café to wait for the remainder of the walkers to join. Once all of us were there, Michele convened the reporting.

"Good morning everyone. I hope you all got to see the magnificent sunrise this morning!"

We all shook our heads yes, and smiled.

"Who would like to begin today?"

Joelle started off, "I am sensing that the necessary pressure has been released in the Alaskan portion of the Ring of Fire, which will eliminate the risk of a major disruption of physical systems. Any remaining backwash pressure along the ley line will be discharged as small tremors."

We were all nodding in agreement.

"Is there anything else that needs to be addressed at this time?" Michele checked in.

When nothing more was offered she directed comments to our interdimensional group, "I want to thank all of you for a particularly potent immersion last night. Your willingness to participate by moving your own blocks was of great service."

With that we concluded the official check-in, and our group slowly dispersed.

I see that Sabrina is talking to Will, who is here in his usual smart attire, at what must be his regular table. He winks at me with one of his twinkling eyes as I pass by.

Kai had arranged to meet Cali at the café after the Earth messenger check-in. They were leaving just ahead of me, and I heard them talking about going over to the communication center to check out the video production equipment. I felt an impulse to go that way as well and just then, a café patron brushed in between us and caught my attention. She said something out of the blue, but by now I knew to pay attention.

"If you like classic movies, they have this for download at the communication center. I suggest you take friends, and then she disappeared into the thin air she seemed to come out of. I looked down at the piece of paper she had slipped into my hand and it read, **The Bridge Over the River, Kai, is Cellular**.

I picked up my pace to catch back up to Kai and Cali.

"Kai, someone just gave me a clue, which appears to be for you and it seems somehow I'm part of it too."

Kai looked at it and under his breath he kept repeating, "The bridge is cellular, the bridge is cellular, the bridge is cellular." As if saying it enough times would surface the meaning.

Cali weighed in saying, "Kai is coming with me, because I am interested in the possibility of using video as a tool for empowering young women and redefining beauty. It's awesome to have you along to help us brainstorm, Chrysalis."

She continued, "I asked Kai to be a part of this process, because I feel that an important part of empowering young women has to do with teaching them to love and respect themselves. The masculine has been dominant, but not empowered... that is not the sacred masculine anyway. The masculine and feminine go hand in hand."

She tenderly reached out and took Kai's hand. "I feel a lot of connection with Kai, and a great deal of respect for how he expresses his male energy. There is a confident, quiet tenderness, which doesn't need to assert itself. When a man is in humble service to the feminine, first and foremost to protect her, he will be gifted beyond his wildest imagination.

When a woman sees and deeply appreciates the gifts of the male, her cup will also be filled. Confidence, mutual respect and self-respect are key to the unfolding and expressed beauty of both of the masculine and feminine aspects. They are intertwined, like a Celtic knot."

"I have to say that what you shared with me yesterday, and what you just said, moved me deeply and I know whatever it is you are going to do will be a powerful gift for young women," I said appreciatively.

"Well, I got a clue to meet someone named Tatiana at the video studio, so I think we are all in for some more interesting unraveling of a larger mystery," Cali beamed. "Shall we?" she asked as she invited us to proceed.

As we continued walking, an image popped up in my mind connected to what Cali had shared. It was an "aha" moment and I blurted out, "Oh my God, Cali, the Celtic knot... the turning scars into beauty... the tattoo I saw you admiring yesterday." I was sort of stammering trying to make the flood of thoughts and words coherent.

"I think I'm with you," she said. "I have been noticing tattoos… you know the way that things seem to show up everywhere, and are almost flashing at you when you are supposed to pay attention?… So, say more."

"Well, when I got my tattoo, I had done an internet search for designs. There was a design that had gone viral at the time of a full-halter tattoo. The woman it was on had gotten it to bring beauty back to her scarred body after a radical mastectomy. The edging on the halter was a chain of Celtic knots that came up around her neck and hung down her back. The main section of the halter was a lush, rainforest ecosystem. It was incredible!"

"Now I know why I am meeting with Tatiana," Cali said excitedly. "Thank you, Chrysalis, for bringing that together for me."

We arrived at the communication center where a tall, slender, exotic looking black woman with long cornrowed hair and blue eyes was standing in the reception area to greet us. "You must be Cali, Kai, and Chrysalis," she offered. "I'm Tatiana…The video bay is open now, so let's go have some fun playing."

"So, what's the goal of your project?" Tatiana asked Cali.

"Well, it started out focused on empowering young girls and redefining beauty, which will still be an outcome, if I do this right. But, now it feels broader… more about all of us just remembering who we really are beyond gender… beyond bodies. It feels like there aren't really words to capture it, like we have to get past mental concepts."

"So what if you don't use words?" Tatiana suggested.

"Well, how do we make an engaging video without words?" Cali wondered.

"Tell a story with movement, images, music, and frequency that creates resonance... Something that awakens cellular memory of who we are and what we are connected to," Tatiana suggested.

Just then Kai's wheels clicked into place. "Oh my God, the bridge is **cellular**! I can bridge the importance of the stories carried by my people through the modern medium of film and video, if I combine the elements in a way that will awaken cellular memory."

"Tell us more," Kai and Cali almost said in unison to Tatiana.

"One of the crises of your time was the 'colony collapse disorder' that threatened the bee population. A pioneering beekeeper, who also worked with subtle energy and frequencies, realized that what the bees needed was to have their hives next to the frequencies of a healthy hive... in order to restore their cellular memory.

She was able to make recordings of the healthiest hives, at different times of year when the hive was in different phases of development. Coincidentally, Kai, the healthy hives were in Hawai'i. She also used special energy tools to strengthen the field and amplify the frequencies. Anyway, her results were impressive... Are you getting where I am going with this?"

All of us were on the edge of our seats and I could see expressions on Kai and Cali's faces like an "aha" was right on the tip of their tongues.

Cali diverted from the frequency piece for a moment and said, "What I'm seeing is images of the scarred Earth, like I was shown yesterday when we visited different sites, overlapping with the images of the restoration and beauty. I see my own body as it is now, and how it can be used as a canvas for a new story to take people through the journey of the pain to the possibility. It has to convey love, respect and hope. I understand how music is an essential part of creating the right tone... is that what you mean by frequency?"

"Music is frequency and, yes, audible music is a key element. There are also powerful frequencies that are not audible to the human ear. At least not with the level of sensory activation you had prior to coming here. For example, the Schumann resonance is a low-level frequency emitted by the Earth, which is beneficial to all life. It is not audible, but it is received and registered by the cells. Actually, the frequency of the bees is a similar, ancient and beneficial resonance. Having these frequency tracks woven into your video can activate alignment with this ancient memory.

Also, for you Kai there is an energy transmission, or frequency, with the traditional chant and hula. When it is carried with reverence it has mana, or life force. That energy comes from the na'au, as your people would say, or the place of inner wisdom or consciousness. It will be captured in the videos."

Kai nodded to affirm what she was saying.

"This is so exciting," Cali shared, "but is it possible to do all this when we go back to our time?"

"Absolutely! There are people who understand these things who will be there to help you."

"Would you like to watch an example, so you can experience what it feels like to be taken deep very quickly?" Tatiana asked. "It's one thing to talk about that kind of experience and it's another thing to have a tangible physically understanding of what it is you are going for."

"For sure," we each said in our various ways as we kicked back in our chairs and she dimmed the lights and cued up the videos.

The first piece was a filming of one of the immersion trance dances. The second one was Polynesian dancers, blended back and forth with the images of the Earth that were depicted in the chant and dance. It was a combination of what Cali and Kai had envisioned.

Tatiana was right. It was important to experience it, because I had never had a video shift me so quickly like that. It took me beyond intellectual processing or commentary and dropped me right into my na'au, as she had described it.

Before we left the communication center, Tatiana handed Cali a card and said, "She's expecting you in about an hour."

Cali looked at the card and smiled. "Hey, Chrysalis, check it out," she said as she turned the card for me to look at:

Rachel Ringwald
Visionary Tattoo Artist
Art Studio 3

"That's so rad!" I said shaking my head like, what's next?

"Hey, will I see you tonight at the open mic?" I added before we headed off in different directions.

"Oh ya…" she said, like she had some surprise up her sleeve.

Kai headed off with her. It seemed that since they connected, they were pretty much joined at the hip. It's cool because they are both such awesome people. I also wondered what was going to happen for them… for all of us… when we go back.

As I got ready to leave the communication center, I noticed the sign on the wall that Luna had texted me about yesterday. It was next to the broadcasting room, where I assumed Michele did her reporting from. Anyway, there was a young guy coming out of there who looked like he was up on this sort of thing.

"Excuse me," I said, pointing to the sign, "do you know about this?"

"Ya, sure," he said, willing to be diverted from whatever task he was involved in.

"So, I went to the Virtua-City site, and I get the social networking part, but I'm curious about what the 'member hosts' do?"

"All of the communities do something different for the engagement experience they create for attendees. When people are hosted here they play the game, just like you are."

I thought to myself, Is it stamped on my forehead or something?… and then I reminded myself, No, it's in my field. Ha!

"Can people use the credits in their transaction accounts in other communities?" I asked.

"Some, but not all. However, there's no charge to attend a gathering, because the point is to encourage in-person participation to create a strong network. Each host community absorbs the gathering costs, but expenses are minimal because people can teleport in, and members with active pages on the site arrange their own accommodations with people they have 'friended' in the hosting community. If there's overflow, we have community members who volunteer to host someone for a couple of nights."

"Wow, I hope I get to attend one someday. It sounds like a great time."

"Ya, it is," he said. "Maybe you'll start one where you are!"

With that, he continued on his way and I continued on mine, although I wasn't clear where I was off to yet. I was feeling so full from all that had happened since I've been here and my mind could use some downtime. I decided to go over to the renewal rooms to see if there was an opening this afternoon. As I headed out the path to the rooms, I noticed something different than the first time I came out here. What I had thought was a bunch of dead sticks lining both sides of the path, now have plump buds on them. I stopped, fascinated by such an interesting plant.

"They are just about to bloom," a middle aged woman commented, who was passing from the opposite direction.

"What kind of plant is it?" I asked curiously.

"Queen of the Desert cactus... It's a big deal when it blooms, since it only happens every few years. The amazing thing about it is that there is some coordinating intelligence, because the blooms that are the fullest and are ready to open wait for the rest. They all have to bloom at the same time to make seeds."

"Does it have a scent?"

"Yes, it's incredibly fragrant. Some say it smells like milk and honey."

"It's blooming soon, you said?" I asked quietly, my thoughts drifting to a connection I sensed.

"Yes, any time."

The woman continued on, and I felt the impulse to lie on the ground next to the plants and to ask them for a little more time. When I got back up, I continued the short distance to the renewal rooms. There was one available. I entered, removed my clothes and slid into the soothing warmth of the tub, feeling the same serenity as the day I had arrived.

The rest of the afternoon slipped by, and it was time to head over to the café for the storytelling experiment Drew had talked me into. I stopped back at my room and changed for the evening, because I wanted to stay for the open mic at 8:00. When I got to the café, Drew was in the back corner setting up a cozy, private space with a table for two. It was covered with a tablecloth that had a pattern of stars and little girls sitting on slivers of moons, fishing for the stars. The only thing that was missing on the table was a crystal ball.

"Hey Drew, are you going to be first?" I said playfully, hoping that he wasn't going to say yes.

"I would, but I have some things I need to do to get the café ready for open mic... I'll have Sabrina let people know you're back here."

"I'm kind of surprised Sabrina is here tonight. I thought she usually worked mornings."

"She does, but she loves open mic nights too."

"Cool," I replied, "I'm always happy to see her."

I settled nervously into my seat, wondering how this whole thing was going to go. Fortunately, I didn't have too much time to think about it before an elder man, in some of the simple clothing many of the residents wear, approached and asked, "Are you open for business?"

Interesting first candidate, I thought to myself.

"Here we don't discount anyone's abilities based on age. I believe you're quite capable and I look forward to receiving your perceptions," he said in transparency-speak.

I laughed to myself thinking, who's reading who here. I also remembered what Drew said about not taking myself too seriously and having fun with the process.

"Absolutely! Have a seat," I offered jovially. "Can I ask your name?"

"Oh, yes, excuse me… I'm Norman."

"Okay Norman…" I said slowly, looking deeply into his eyes to explore what wanted to be seen. "You recently lost someone dear to you…"

Wait a second I thought, that's not light and fun. Then I heard, "Just go with it."

"She said you forgot to put the cap back on the toothpaste this morning and that she's not going anywhere until you are ready to go with her. She also said, no rush because she's having a perfectly good time hanging out with you this way. She just wants you to enjoy yourself…"

I saw a sparkle come back into his dimming eyes, as he said, "Putting the cap back on the toothpaste was the one thing she never could get me to remember to do. Ha!"

He seemed satisfied with our interaction and he got up for the next person, which was Sage. She looked different than the way I had first perceived her. She was more integrated with her body, and her look had changed from academic intelligence to whole-being awareness.

"Hey Sage, it's great to see you here. I was just thinking the other day that I hadn't had enough time to connect with you one-on-one."

"Ya, I was thinking the same."

"Okay, well let's have some fun playing… So, as an only child of parents who are academics, there was a lot of expectation on you to follow in some kind of intellectual pursuit. You have a strong, inquisitive mind, so that wasn't an issue, but you are also very intuitive and because of that you sometimes seemed irrational in your choices. You have an unexpressed trickster in you that you haven't been able to find a way to bring forward, since your family tends to be very serious and doesn't find humor or lightheartedness appropriate when there is so much suffering in the world. You operate more from your heart than your mind, and that will end up enabling you to make an incredible scientific breakthrough related to a technological device for healthcare."

Sage was silent for a moment and then said, "It feels good to be in a place where so many people see and get me. I had cut off important parts of myself... imagination, intuition and playfulness... and it feels good to reclaim them. The details in your story weren't exactly right, but the gist of it was right on... Do you mind if I say what I get about you?"

"No, not at all."

"You are learning to trust that the universe will support you, because up until the past couple of years it seemed you were the kid at the candy store window... you could look, but you weren't invited in to buy. You have amazing gifts for seeing what doesn't work in the world and using your words to turn pain into possibility for something new. When you speak, people will listen, so use your words well."

"Thank you, Sage. It's good to know you."

"Likewise... We're all in this together."

There were a couple more people after Sage and then Zander took the chair.

"Hey Zander, welcome to Fantasy Island where your secret personas can be played out," I chuckled friskily, now fully in the swing with my "seer" character.

"It's been great watching how much you have come into your own since you arrived. You remind me of someone who always made me laugh to lighten heavy situations. You have a quality like the Dalai

Lama—a childlike innocence that brings joy to an imperfect world. I think your social awkwardness came from being around people who were tiptoeing around your 'condition' and not wanting to talk about it. It was easier for them to keep you out of social situations and you picked up on their energy. You have an off-beat sense of humor that could not only help you in difficult situations, but could also help people open up to new ways of seeing things. I encourage you to develop it."

"I'm pretty shy, so what makes you think I'm funny?"

"Just a guess. I don't claim to be right."

"I had always thought that my attempts at humor would just be more cause for people to make fun of me. I appreciate your seeing it as a possible asset."

"That's awesome, Zander. I hope I'll have a chance to experience that side of you before we leave."

I saw Drew give me the wrap up signal, since the open mic was ready to begin. Zander and I relocated to better seats for viewing the performances.

First up was a guitar and flute duo. Then, to my surprise, Zander stood up and took the stage.

"Hey everybody, how are you all doing tonight?" he began tentatively.

Various responses of great, good, awesome came back.

"So, where I came from, I guess I could be called socially awkward. I'd try to go to the parties and act like I was having fun, but I could never pull it off. People just thought I was having a pretend-excitis attack.

185

I have to tell you I loved my entry here. It was more like a sedimental journey than the airport security I was used to. Last time I was in an airport, the TSA guard asked if she had permission to wand me. I said, 'Only if you promise that all of my dreams will come true.' I guess that system wasn't so bad after all, because obviously it worked.

What's great here too, is that I don't have to stress about exams. I can just pick the brain of the guy next to me.

You know, there are so many things here to have fun doing that I could get distracted from the seriousness of answering my question. So, I remind myself of the line from the Lord's Prayer I learned as a child, 'Lead us not into temptation, but deliver us some E-mail.'... Ha! Of course that's just another distraction, but maybe I'll find some good clues there.

Anyway, this has been an incredible experience. Thank you for helping me to see the power of joy and laughter to create a better world by breaking the tension around what we don't know how to speak about... May the farce be with you!"

Right on, Zander, I thought to myself as I looked around and saw an ocean of appreciative smiles and people chuckling. I also noticed that all of the interdimensionals were here tonight. It feels like a pre-graduation celebration, and I am grateful for the time with these amazing people.

Next to take the stage was Cali. She had on a pair of white leggings and a white high-low tank top that flowed with the gracefulness of her stride. It wasn't her beautiful, tan skin that was set off by the simple outfit, but rather the tattoo I could see coming up from under her top and continuing around her neck. It was a chain of Celtic knots, as I had described to her.

She stepped to the mic and said, "I want to thank Ariel for taking me on a journey of a lifetime yesterday. We visited places on the Earth that had been badly damaged and I witnessed the love and creativity that had restored them to a new kind of beauty.

I write a form of ten-syllable poetry called Dekaaz, which I am going to weave together with dance to celebrate my own restoration."

She placed the mic off the stage, easily able to project what she needed to speak in the intimate setting.

"Sacred
this body
that is of the Earth."

She spoke with a full and reverent resonance, as she slowly drew her palms up her beautifully defined legs, catching the hem of her top and pulling it over her head to reveal the full-halter tattoo. She dropped the garment in front of her and continued. Her beginning movements were gentle, fluid and cradling like those of a mother strolling to introduce the world to her new child.

"Forest
still heals me
despite her own wounds."

"The Earth
uses me
to feel her longing."

The strength and power of her breathtaking, expressive flow gave body language a whole new meaning, as she transformed the stage into a chalice into which we all poured our hearts.

"Pity
keeps beauty
from showing its face."

"See me
strong enough
to rise to the call."

She danced as if she were calling the wind into her service. It blew through us like a gust through an old house, knocking the yellowing family photo from its assigned place. It was a welcome disturbance that brought freshness to what had become stale.

"You see
suffering,
I know only grace."

"I am
not damaged
I am so much more."

"Beauty
speaks respect
as the name it wears."

When she finished, you could have heard a pin drop. Slowly, everyone caught their breath again and, one-by-one, rose until the whole room was standing.

At the end of all of the performances, I made my way over to Kai and Cali. Others were also stopping to say how moved they were by what she did. I haven't been much of a huggy person in my life, but tonight I wanted that kind of touch from everyone. Cali and Kai both felt it from me and gave me the sandwich version of an embrace.

"Wow, Cali, you blew me away... the tattoo's amazing... you're amazing!"

"Thanks," was all she said.

"How did they do something so complex that quickly?" I asked in awe of the tattoo.

"It's incredible what they can do with digital technology now. We found the image you described and the tattoo artist basically copied it onto my body. It's temporary because Rachel said it wouldn't stay with me when I go back, but I can recreate a permanent one there."

CHAPTER 15

The Returning

As I walked to the path this morning to join the Earth messengers, I had the sense that my journey on the infinity loop would soon be ending. There were more people than usual on the path to the renewal rooms at this hour. I could see that many were snapping photos and there was a celebratory feel to the activity. Getting closer, I saw that the Queen of the Desert plants had all bloomed.

I continued on past the flora festivities to meet the Earth messengers. My connection to the Earth, and what she had to share, felt particularly strong this morning. There was a bitter sweetness to it. As I walked the loop and extended fingers to touch those of the intersecting walkers, what I noticed was electricity arcing between us, more than I had felt before. A sense of grace... that all was well... washed over me. I also had a vague memory of having been on the sending end of that message to someone when I came here. It occurred to me that my time on the infinity loop was not ending. I just hadn't realized how far it stretched.

Back at the café, Michele brought our convening to order. Today, in addition to the regular Earth messengers, she had requested the remainder of the interdimensionals to join us.

"As I'm sure you are all aware, the Queen of the Desert is blooming. This is a reminder that it's time to gather your seeds and to go back and plant them. Take them far and wide, nurture them and have patience, knowing that it may be a while before the seeds are ready to harvest again.

Remember, the same universe you have come to trust and to know here as a playful companion, exists where you are going. It's just that when the mind is in fear you can't see it. The energy of **this** place lives inside of you and you take it with you everywhere. You can't lose it. Also know that there are people like you, who have come here ahead of you. They will be there to support you.

The most important thing to know is that you are not leaving the game. Going back is not so much about what you will **do**, as it is about how you will **be** as a result of your time here. You've learned how to navigate the game... how to relax, be present and to listen for what you need related to your questions. You don't have to worry about putting it all together into a plan for what you **will do** because that takes you out of the powerful **now** and you will miss important information.

There is a divine intelligence that has an investment in this **with you, that is you,** and it is the same intelligence that creates worlds. When you are in alignment with it, what you need shows up in perfect timing. Enjoy being in the process. Remember that no matter how serious the circumstances feel that you find yourselves in, hold them lightly and you will be given access to a greater range of possibilities.

Some of you are wondering how you will find each other again. There is some blurring of full memory when you return, but you will recognize each other by your frequencies. You will feel familiar to each other, or you might think that someone reminds you of another person. The essence of you doesn't change, although our physical bodies do, even in one lifetime. How you appear at five years old is quite different than the body you will occupy at eighty, but you always know yourself as the same life force.

All of you, in your unique ways, are part of keeping the sacred story alive. Thank you for your courage and perseverance in claiming your own authority over your lives and using your gifts fully. Trevor will make the arrangements with each of you today to return as you came."

Michele completed her address to the interdimensionals and returned to the business of the Earth messenger check-in.

"Has anyone detected any disturbances that need to be discussed today?"

All heads indicated, no.

Cameron was sitting next to Zander and I heard him say, "The picture of what you knew was possible got you here. When you go back, create a new picture of where you want to see yourself in that reality and focus on it. I see you as an advocate for helping others who have been labeled as autistic spectrum to bring their gifts forward. You may even play an important role in early warning systems for natural disasters, if you choose."

Everyone was hanging out in the area, sharing their appreciation with each other and with members of the community who had come to offer their best wishes.

I moved over to where Trevor was standing and asked, "Could I talk to you for a minute?" indicating I would like to go off to the side, away from of the active conversation.

"Yes, of course."

We found a spot not far from the rest, but enough to give us an uninterrupted moment.

"I've known you such a short time, but I feel like I've always known you," I said softly.

"We have traveled together before, and we will travel together again," he affirmed lovingly, as he wrapped me in the strength of his tender arms.

He continued, "Can you be ready to go by 1:00?"

I swallowed hard and waited for the word to come, "Yes."

"Good. I'll meet you at the labyrinth."

I nodded and returned to the group, wanting to spend the rest of my time here with them. There was no reason to go back to my guestroom anyway, since I couldn't take anything back with me. The time passed quickly, with Sage and Luna leaving the group ahead of me.

Then it was my turn, and I made my way out to the labyrinth about twenty minutes before 1:00 so I could walk it once again. Trevor showed up right on time and I got into the transport vehicle with him, feeling a great deal of peace.

When we got just outside the community, he cloaked the vehicle and said to me, "So, do you want to drive?"

"Sure!" I chuckled, thinking this could make learning to drive a car interesting.

He entered a few codes on the command panel and then took the TD I would no longer be needing and dropped it into the control bay, so the vehicle would respond to me. "Remember, in manual it is completely thought responsive."

"Okay, cowboy, hold on!"

With that I thought, I'm ready to soar and I envisioned the starlings again, but not in a flock. Rather, the way they would daringly swoop down at top speed hugging the surface of cliffs, or other objects, and then pulling up at the last moment. It was effortless, thrilling, and required full presence and attention. It was a great way to conclude our time together and we were both laughing uproariously when we arrived at the pool on the canyon floor under the Grand Staircase.

"I'm going to leave you and let you have your privacy in the pool. When you're ready to be taken back through the wormhole, just tune into the love in your heart and say, **Now**."

I nodded and didn't look as he turned to get back in the transport vehicle.

I took off the clothing I had on and stepped into the shallow pool, yielding my body to water and the Earth. I wanted to go back the same way I came in, naked and innocent... "**Now**."

The iridescent plasma encased me, as I sensed moving at great speed. The images of so many times and faces came at a pace where I could register each story in a pool of unconditional love, regardless of the nature of the images. Then everything went dark for a millisecond and I had stopped moving.

I was aware of being in a cold, steel frame bed with instruments beeping. There was a harsh light on my eyelids. I opened them slowly to adjust to the bright flatness of the light in the room. There was no sweet scent of blossoms in the air, only the smell of rubbing alcohol and latex. I felt a hand on mine and I looked over to see Bree standing there.

"The hospital phoned me and told me you might be coming out of the coma, so I came right away."

194

"How long have I been gone?"

"Ten days."

"You look so beautiful, Chrysalis, even in that tacky hospital gown," she said in the playful way that I remembered.

"Thanks for calling me Chrysalis and thanks for being here... You've been there haven't you?"

"Yes, but differently than you. If we talk in terms of **time**, I would say **I came back from the future** you just experienced **to be of assistance now.** I was a member of the community, whereas you came as a visitor. But really there is only **now** and the many dreams are happening simultaneously, as you discovered.

I never told you about my spending time as a part of a dolphin swim community. I went, as so many do, in search of the **field** of love, joy and playfulness **they collectively create.** After being with the dolphins for only a brief time, they showed me an image of a kindergarten class with many children who were delighting in hanging out with the teacher. The children loved it so much that they never wanted to leave, yet more and more children were coming and the teacher got to the point where she could no longer handle all of their needs. The dolphins communicated that what they hoped was that some of us would **get** what they were creating... to claim who we really are, which is love, and to learn to create the field among ourselves."

"I understand," I said, still basking in the energy of that same loving field, which I had just come back through. "Bree, I know why I'm here."

"Good."

"...and I need to find my father."

"I know. He and I both entered this experience with the same level of understanding, but he got caught up in the idea of separation and gave into the fear."

"I remember your explaining to people about how you could work remotely with quantum biofeedback, because there is no separation in the field. Now I get what that means."

"Indeed, we are all in this together!"

About the Author

Dawn Griffin has spent her adult life following guidance to answer the question, "Who are we really and how do we realize our greatest potential?" That quest has led her to exploring a range of disciplines, as a way to hold a larger picture of a thriving, interconnected whole. She holds a bachelor's degree in Environmental Policy and Planning and has worked in the field of optimal human health as a quantum biofeedback practitioner.

In the late 90s, she created an uplifting, multi-image show for a conference on spirituality and the environment to highlight positive approaches being offered for many of the social and environmental issues we face. That presentation, entitled, *On Wings of a Dream,* was later transferred to a video format and distributed.

Her adventures have taken her from a small coral atoll in the South Pacific to a journey across Siberia. Currently, her primary focus is writing and storytelling. She returns periodically to her childhood home in Denver, Colorado to reconnect with family.

CPSIA information can be obtained at www.ICGtesting.com
Printed in the USA
BVOW05s0942120814

362497BV00001B/111/P